A Savage and His Lying Tongue

THE SAVAGE SERIES
BOOK TWO

L L MOMON

Truth is stranger than fiction, but it is because Fiction is obliged to stick to possibilities; Truth isn't.

— MARK TWAIN

Trigger Warning

This book contains content that may be disturbing to some. Topics addressed include domestic violence, abuse, explicit sexual content, and foul language. Readers discretion is advised.

Contents

Acknowledgements

As always, I would like to thank God because he is first and foremost the head of my life. I would also like to thank each and every person that has taken the time to purchase any one of my books in any format. I truly appreciate each and every one of you. To the people who encourage me to continue honing my craft, I thank you. The encouragement is much obliged. I started this for me but I continue it for me and you. To my friends and family. You are loved and thank you tremendously for your support. Stay up and Be Blessed.

Dedication

I want to dedicate this book to all the men who are loving and treating their women properly. The men that go above and beyond in doing whatever it takes to make their woman happy. I once came across a quote that said, "You can tell a lot about a man by the size of the smile on his woman's face." This statement couldn't be truer. When a women is loved correctly, it shows. She walks different, she moves different and she think differently. She glows. Keep making her glow. In fact, turn that glow into a high beam if you can. She and God will love you just that much more for it.

"Love your wife as God loved the Church." In case you didn't know. That is immeasurable.

Author's Note

Hold up!! Before you crack this book open, please make sure that you have read book one in the Savage series. A Savage and Her Wicked Ways. This book, A Savage and His Lying Tongue, is the second installment in the Savage Series. This book provides the backstory of the toxic relationship between Taji's mother Jordan and her father Indigo. It also provide more insight on his disappearance, how Taji was raised and the events that took place in her childhood. I mean' Taji had to get those toxic ways from somewhere. If you are curious about the who's, why's and when's of the first savage. This book is the answer. This is not a standalone so to get everything that is suppose to be gave, please stop and read book one first. Smooches.

Also by L L Momon

Whittling Wood Book 1

Whittling Wood Book 2

A Savage and Her Wicked Ways

The Sweetest Symphony, A Savage's Apprentice /Coming Soon

To Love the Broken and Unhealed/Coming Soon

The Hardest of Hearts/Coming Soon

"Play your hand and don't try any funny shit either. I know how you young bucks like to get down. Y'all niggas love to cheat and we ain't having that shit here." I muttered while slamming the high joker on the table.

"Man, your ass must can't count or something. Ain't nobody cheating. Don't get pissed at me because you and your bitch are losing!" Solo quipped as he sucked his teeth while cuffing his cards closer to his body. He studied his hand before throwing out another.

Not believing my ears, I scoffed. "Nigga, I beg your pardon. Come again... I need you to repeat that." Sneering, I lowered my hands below the table.

"You heard what the fuck I said, O.G. I ain't gotta repeat shit. Tell that bitch of yours to play her cards right and you won't have to worry about the score. We are not cheating. That bitch------"

WHOP, WHOP, WHOP, CRACK... was the sound heard immediately after the last *bitch* rolled off his lips. Nobody in the house moved or said a word.

"Now, one of you youngsters come get him up and y'all ain't worth a shit. What kind of homeboys are y'all? You should have warned him about who he was fucking with. I hate when niggas come from up north and try to act hard. Thinking that because we are in the south that we are slow and don't know how to handle ourselves. I bet his ass learned today."

"Damn, Indigo, he's just a jit. You didn't have to fuck him up like that." Tick voiced as he shook Solo, attempting to wake him up.

"Tick, you are talking about fucking him up. If he didn't come to my house talking shit then we wouldn't have had shit to worry about. He's lucky that breaking his arm and pistol whipping him was all that I did. I should have taken those raggedy run down Timberland boots that he's wearing and shoved them up his ass. I'm gonna let him breathe though. I don't have any more energy to waste on a nobody like him. I'm trying to enjoy my night."

"Aye, Aye, Solo!!!! Wake your bitch ass up," I yelled. I slapped him across the face a few times, trying to get him to come to, but he was acting like I'd put a slug through his ass. Finally, he cracked his eyes open and slowly sat up. "Can you hear me, lil nigga? Are your ears working? Don't tell me that you went deaf on me."

Solo looked around, blurry eyed as if he didn't know where he was.

Snapping my fingers, I demanded that he wake the fuck up. "I need for you to apologize to my wife. Don't you *ever* fix your mouth to disrespect her again and if you dream that you did, you better wake up apologizing."

"Ummm, what? What happened?" Solo muttered in a confused tone.

"Nevermind what happened. I suggest you apologize before it happens again."

In a haste, he perked up and mumbled, "I apologize, ma'am. I am sorry."

"That ain't good enough!! Tell her what you are sorry for!!" I yelled.

"Indigo, he said he was sorry. You always do too much," Jordan said as she pushed my head to the side. "You didn't have to do all that."

"But I did, Jordan, now be quiet and let the man apologize to you the proper way. Say it, lil nigga, before I break my foot off in your ass again!!!" Solo sat all the way up, attempting to shake away the pain and fully understand what was happening.

His voice shaking and full of fear, he blurted out,

"Ma'am, I am sorry for calling you out of your name. It will never happen again and Mr. Indigo, I apologize to you, too."

"Apology accepted. Now y'all get him the fuck out of here and don't ever bring him back."

I can't and could never stand disrespectful youngins. To see a young nigga talk shit to his elders pissed me off like no other. I wasn't trying to punk him, I was just trying to show him that you can't fuck with everyone like that. Somebody should have taught him better manners. Next time, he might not run into somebody as nice as me.

"Aye, Tick. Man, can you find somebody else to play his hand? I'm trying to enjoy a nice game night with my family and you all brought this damn riffraff over here."

Everyone acted as if they were scared to move besides Tick. Tick and I had been rolling together since hush was a puppy and blood couldn't make us any closer. I employed a list of soldiers in my camp but only one Lieutenant and that was Tick. He was the *go to* whenever I wasn't available, which was kind of often. While I was out running the streets and chasing bitches, Tick was busy chasing the bag. My nigga was truly about his business in every sense of the word.

Standing up and turning his fitted cap to the back, Tick yelled out, "Somebody sit down and play the damn hand. There ain't shit to be scared of. All you have to do is sit down, play, and shut the fuck up. It's not hard."

A nickel and dimed hustler named Shalimar, Mar-Mar for short, sat down and grabbed Solo's cards.

"I'll play his hand, Indigo. Shit, I've been trying to get close to you all night. I need to talk to you about something but it can wait until later. Seeing that your wife and daughter are here, I know that you'd prefer not to talk business around them."

"Mar, or whatever it is that you call yourself, I'm sure that there isn't shit that you and I need to talk about. Whatever you are thinking about, you can speak to Tick about it. I'm busy and not trying to hear that shit." I said as I turned my attention to my wife.

"Sweets, would you please fix me a Hennessy on the rocks? Please and I only need two ice cubes."

Always Slidin'

JORDAN

I got up and trekked to the kitchen to fix Indigo a drink. My friends, Sonia and Sage, were at the table whispering like two messy ass old ladies.

"What are you two whores in here snickering about?" I queried as I pranced through the door.

"Girl, now why did you sit your ass there and let Indigo beat the shit out of that man?" Sage asked as she took a drink of her Maddog 20/20.

"I was about to say something but before I could get a word out, he'd already snapped his arm. What in the hell was I supposed to do? You all know how he gets when someone says or does something that he doesn't like. There is no stopping him. I know one thing, I bet he won't call nobody else *a bitch* without thinking twice."

Sonia and Sage looked at each other and cracked up laughing.

"Shidddd, us either," Sonia laughed. "If Solo knew like we knew, he would stay his ass from around here. Indigo don't let shit slide. He is liable to beat that man's ass every time that he sees him," they all agreed while cackling.

"Anyway, hand me the Hennessy," I ordered as I reached for a glass. "Let me get this drink to him so that he can go ahead and leave. Then I can get some rest. I know that he's going out tonight. He's going to act like he isn't, but I know that his ass is going to book it out that front door the minute that he gets a chance. He's out there talking about he's spending time with his family. Hummmph, this isn't family time. We are out here playing this boring ass card game while my baby is in her room. Unfortunately, that is where Taji will stay while all these different men are in this house. He knows that I don't play having just anyone around her. She's a little girl and I don't trust anybody when it comes to my one and only."

"We don't blame you, girl. You know what happened to my niece last year. My sister won't let her stay at anybody's house anymore," Sage chimed.

"Jordan, what's taking so long? Do I have to come in there and fix the drink myself? Can you please hurry up so we can finish this game and get these niggas out of this house?"

"I'll be back in a minute, ladies. It shouldn't be much longer now." I fixed the drink and headed back out to the card table where Indigo and his friends were.

"Thank you, Sweets. I didn't mean to rush you like that, but I've got to cut a few corners tonight." He casually threw that out while he took a sip from his glass.

My lips balled up involuntarily. "You're welcome and I already knew that you were going out. I just told the girls. I don't know why you are always trying to play with me like I don't know you like the back of my hand. You are so predictable that it isn't even funny anymore. You always have somewhere to be despite you saying that we would spend quality time together."

"Ahhh, come on, Jordan. Please don't start that shit tonight. I have all the time in the world to spend with you and Taji. Besides, my little babygirl understands that her daddy has to make moves. Shidd, if you weren't such a helicopter mom, I'd take her with me sometimes."

"No the hell you wouldn't. You will not be exposing my daughter to those ghetto birds that you like to hang with. She's just a little girl, Indigo. She's barely eight years old."

"Jordan, don't you know by now that our baby has been here before. My grandma told me when she was born that she was an old soul. She's been in the mix long enough to know what's up. You know kids are way smarter than we give them credit for."

"Yeah, I know but I still think that it's good to keep some things private from them. Especially the type of shit that you do. I don't need her thinking that any of it is ok because it isn't. She's super impressionable at this age, Indigo."

"I get it, Jordan, but can we please talk about this another time? It's hard for me to play this hand and have a serious conversation. I promise that we will talk about it later."

"Whatever. I'm going to go check on Taji." I sucked my teeth and I got up and walked away.

Be My Peace

INDIGO

"On everything, I love my old lady. Having a wife and family is cool and all but I damn sure hate having to answer to her ass. You see how she be on my ass, man, and she don't let up either." I admit to Tick and Melee.

"Sometimes, it feels like I'm doing time all over again. I love the fuck out of her though. She's about the only person on this earth that can say the shit that she says to me and get away with it."

Melee was another soldier in my camp, but he hadn't been around nearly as long as Tick. He and I crossed paths when I served a short prison sentence at the Alabama Department of Corrections.

I was well-known around those parts as a big dog, and I took Melee under my wing after some niggas got at him in the yard one day. After he finished his stint, Melee was released and immediately got up with me to see if I had any work for him. I did and he was now my glorified do-boy and was in charge of handling my light weight.

"Aye, Tick, when she comes back out, I'm going to need for you to say that you need to dip so that I can get the fuck out of here. I've got a lil bop waiting for me across town and I'm not trying to miss the opportunity to slide through and see her fine ass."

"Indigo, I told you that bitch wasn't shit. The only reason that Imani and those other bitches fuck with you is because you on right now. If you didn't have shit, that bitch wouldn't even look your way. Plus, isn't she a lil young for you?"

"Tick, mind your muthafucking business and just do like I asked. Yeah, she's a lil young but she's *all* woman. Shidd, if you knew the things that she did to me then you would understand why I fuck with her." I laughed and elbowed Tick in the side. He didn't find that shit amusing and waved off my gesture. He was a simp for these bitches and he could think what he wanted. Jordan was my wife and main lady but ain't no way that God gave us all this sperm for just one pussy.

"Anyway, who said that it was Imani? I got a slew of bitches that I can hit anytime I want. Imani is just the front runner, nigga," I offered as I ran my fingers through my goatee.

"Yo ass is almost 40 years old with a beautiful wife and a kid. *She* should be the front runner. Jordan is smart, beautiful, and most of all, loyal. She loves your trifling ass and would follow you to the end of the world and you are going to jeopardize it for a slut like Imani? Shit, couldn't be me," he expressed through gritted teeth.

"That's right, nigga, it couldn't be you because it's *me*. I'm *him*. I'm that nigga and what I do or don't do with my wife is none of your muthafucking business. I don't say shit when you are over at the spot cuddled up with a different bitch every other night. I don't judge you, so don't judge me."

"That's different, Indigo. You are married. I'm not. I'm single as a one-dollar bill so I can do what I please with no guilt. Those chicks come chill with me and when I leave the spot, I take my ass home. Alone. I'm not down bad about any of these bitches like you are but you are right. It's none of my business so keep that shit in mind when you need me to cover for your ass." Tick sat back in his chair. A scowl was etched across his face. My nigga was passionate as fuck about something that had nothing to do with him. He would understand one day though.

Jordan trekked back in the room and sat down at the table. I eyeballed Tick, trying to signal him to say something, but he didn't utter a word. He sat there, ignoring me, slapping his card to the table. I attempted to kick him to get his attention but ended up kicking Jordan instead.

"Owwwwww. What the hell was that? Who just kicked me? That shit hurt," she whined as she bent down to rub her shin.

"My bad, baby, I didn't mean to do that. I caught a charley horse in my leg and I was trying to kick it out. I'm sorry. Ummm, anyway, baby, we've got to bounce. I'm going to go drop Tick off at home. Then I am heading over to Mason's to shoot a few games of pool. I'll be back later."

Jordan cut her eyes at me, and I knew that she was about to go off. In three, two, one.

"Why can't you drop them off and come back home? You just couldn't wait to get your ass out of here, could you? I knew it. Every Friday night like clockwork, you are gone. You could at least pretend that you want to be home with me and Taji sometimes. Do you ever consider that I may want to go out with my girls every now and again?"

"Well go, Jordan," I shrugged. "I'm not stopping you. You are the one that act like you don't want to go anywhere or do anything."

"Is that really what you think? You think I like sitting up in this house every weekend watching *In The Heat Of The Night* and *Dateline*," she asked. "No, nigga, I don't, but we have a small kid and no one that I trust to watch her. If I'm out and you are out, then who's going to keep an eye on her? Did you ever stop and ask yourself that question?"

"To be honest, Jordan, no I didn't and I'm not about to start tonight. I'm just going to make a few moves and I'll be back home. Damn, you don't have to trip every time that I walk out the door. Why don't you and your girl-friends in there watch a movie or something or go get some more wine for y'all to drink on? Here's some money," I handed her a crisp one-hundred-dollar bill. "Shit, do anything but talk shit at me because I'm tired of hearing it."

"Fuck that. I'm good and you can keep your money. I'm not one of those other bitches. You can't buy me," she scoffed as she tried to put it back in my hand. I wouldn't accept it.

"What I will do is get everyone out of here so that I can spend quality time with our babygirl since you don't want to. As a matter of fact, don't say shit else to me, Indigo. Just go and cut your corners or cut that bitch. Whichever you decide, I hope you enjoy."

My beeper went off, startling us both. I glanced down at my belt, silenced the noise, and didn't mutter another word. Jordan shook her head in disgust and walked back towards the kitchen where Sonia and Sage were. I knew she was pissed but wasn't she always? I snapped my fingers, Tick and Melee stood up and began walking towards the door. Tick looked back, cracked a smile, and waved goodbye to her and the ladies. Melee walked out first, Tick second, and me last, slamming the door on my way out. I was tired of her always running her mouth. She wasn't ever satisfied, and nothing was ever enough for her. Shit, I was going where I could get some peace and it damn sure wasn't here.

Light Over Darkness

JORDAN

"Jordan, did you see how Tick's fine ass just looked at you? What's up with that?" Sage asked.

"I didn't see shit. Tick is cool and all, but he would never step to me. Indigo would have his head, but I'm not gonna lie. That muthafucka is fine and always has been, with his high yellow ass. Anyway, I'm not worried about Tick. I'm still on Indigo's ass. I'm so sick of that nigga's shit. He thinks I'm stupid. I know that he's going to see some bitch and when I find out who she is, I'm fucking the both of them up!! He's not about to have me around town looking dumb."

"Too late," Sage whispered.

"What in the fuck do you mean *too late*, Sage? I heard that shit."

"I mean, I thought that you already knew. Hell, *everybody else* does. I heard that he was fucking with some bitch over there in the Saxton Projects. I don't know her name, but I can call around and find out for you," Sage offered.

"Oh, forreal? And how long did you two bitches know before you decided to open your mouths tonight?"

"Wait, Jordan, I didn't know anything just like you, so please don't include me in this mess," Sonia pleaded.

"Ummm, ummm..." Sage stuttered. "I wanted to tell you but it's really none of my business. You know how women can get when you tell them about their man. I wasn't trying to fuck up our friendship over some *he said, she said*," she offered as she took another swig of her drink.

"Sage, I'm not the kind of person to persecute you for looking out for me. Those other bitches might like to play dumb but not me. I like to know what I'm dealing with at all times. You know what? I should put you the fuck out, but I can see why you didn't say shit. You are right, some women do trip when you tell them about their man but I'm not some women. Just know, you can always come to me when you see some shit that isn't right."

"Now, I've got to get my babygirl situated and get this house back in order so I will catch up with you all tomorrow. Sage, when we talk again, you better have a name for me or you can forget mine."

Grabbing her keys, Sage stretched out her arms for a

hug, but I bobbed and weaved as if I was in a boxing match.

I let out a sigh and put both hands up. "Ummm, no, Sage. I love you and all, but I'm pissed right now so please don't put your hands on me. I am liable to two piece your ass. I need you to grab your shit and go. Oh, and Sage, don't forget your bottle of Maddog 20/20. Nobody in this house drinks that shit but you. Please take it with you," I stated as I walked them to the door. Grabbing Sonia around the neck, I hugged her and told her that I would call her tomorrow and saw them out.

As the house grew quiet, I began throwing away the empty beer bottles and emptying the ashtrays. I got my house back in order before retreating to Taji's room to spend a little time with her.

"Mommy, I've been waiting for you to come in and get me." Taji perked up as I pranced through her door.

"Well, here I am, little miss Taji. It's just you and me. It's late and time for you to go to bed but we can watch a movie until the sandman finds you. Why don't you pick out something to watch while I go in the kitchen to pop us some popcorn?"

"Mommy, I already have it ready to play. Let's watch *Cinderella*. You know that it's my favorite movie," Taji confessed.

"Go ahead and put it on and I'll be right back."

After watching *Cinderella* with Taji for the hundredth time, I eased out of her bed and quietly slipped out of the room. Sighing at the thought of going to sleep alone once again for the third time this week, I turned on my brand-new flat screen tv. Then I opened a window and plopped down onto the bed. Reaching on the nightstand, I retrieved a blunt from the ashtray and put fire to it.

As the smoke filled my lungs, I closed my eyes and let the bud put me in a state of complete relaxation. I loved getting high to ease my mind but hated that it made me so horny. Especially when Indigo wasn't around to scratch that itch.

The horniness didn't go away just because he wasn't there, so I was forced to come up with ways to please myself. Indigo was against having any kind of sexual toys in the household. Something about there wasn't nothing running up in his woman but him. Because of that, my fingers and I became well acquainted.

I put the blunt down and tiptoed over to the bathroom to clean my hands. I stripped naked and climbed back into the bed, fantasizing about the big dick slingers in the books that I would read from time to time. I started with caressing my breasts and sliding my fingers across my nipples until they tightened and hardened like little chocolatey mountains. I sucked and licked my fingers before making my way down to my hotspot. I teased myself by gently stroking my clit up and down until I felt the pressure begin to build. Pulling back the hood of my clit, I licked my fingers and took a deep dive into my pussy. I was so wet that my fingers slid in with ease. Indigo always told me that I walked around with a fire hydrant between my legs. That was at least one thing that he didn't lie about.

I rotated my fingers around my pussy slowly at first and then turned it up a notch. I felt a tingling sensation and I knew that my release wasn't far away. With the other hand, I stuck two fingers deep into my yoni and finger fucked myself until I had no choice but to let go. The combination made me shudder and recoil. By the end of it, I was in a fetal position, almost breathless. I grabbed the towel that lied next to me and wiped my fingers clean before picking the blunt back up and putting fire to it again. This time the smoke took me away to a time where there was more light than darkness.

One of the Good Ones

"**G**ood morning, Mrs. Perry. Are you going to eat for me today? Shanika told me that she was trying to get you to eat all day yesterday and you refused."

"Well, baby, that young lady be going too fast. She shovels food in my mouth and gets my clothes all messed up. Then she wipes my face too hard, and I don't like it. Hell, I don't like *her*. I'd rather wait until you come. I like when you feed me. You take your time."

"Ok, Mrs. Perry, I will be sure to let her know to take it slow with you. Now open up because I've got 2 more to feed right after you."

Just as I placed a towel around her neck and grabbed the first spoon of food, the door cracked open.

"Hey, Grandma, it's good to see you up and eating.

The charge nurse told me that you have been refusing to eat your dinner, but I see that you are getting down this morning," he grinned.

"Hey, Gogo, I'm so glad to see you, baby. I knew it was you when the door opened because you are the only one that comes to see me. You make sure to tell your sisters that I said they can kiss my ass."

He laughed, "Grandma, don't be like that. They are busy with work and kids so don't be too hard on them. I will deliver the message though. Oh, hello ma'am, I'm Indigo," he announced as he reached his hand out to mine for a handshake.

"I'm sorry. I would shake your hand but as you can see, they are kind of full. I'm Jordan and it's nice to meet you."

"Jordan, this is my oldest and favorite grandbaby. I practically raised him. Look at him. Isn't he handsome?"

Fuck yeah, he's handsome and he smells good enough to eat. Look at those pretty white teeth and that smile. Shit, all I see is trouble.

Lying through my teeth, I offered. "To be honest, Mrs. Perry, I hadn't really noticed," I chimed as I continued spooning the grits into Mrs. Perry's mouth.

"Well, baby, you should look up. My grandbaby is one of the good ones. He's got his own business. He's 30 years old, single, and he doesn't have any children. I'd say that he is a good catch. Oh, and most importantly of all, he was raised right. I know this because *I'm* the one that raised him," she laughed as she chewed her grits while I gently wiped her mouth.

"Grandma, do you have to tell all of my business? I doubt if she cares about me and what I do. I came in here to check on my favorite girl, and you are in here trying to play matchmaker."

"Gogo, this young lady takes great care of me so let me brag on her for a minute. I don't want for nothing as long as she's around. She really cares about her patients and loves on us. She's sweet and is always sneaking me little treats. Now Gogo, she hasn't been here that long, but I hope that she isn't quick to leave either. This nursing home needs more people like her. The rest of these heifers are just here to get a damn check. They don't really care if my ass is clean or not."

Indigo and I cackled. Indigo and his grandmother began chopping it up. He told her about his morning, and she did the same. I observed how attentive he was to her, and it warmed my heart. I didn't see that very often with visitors. I'd only been working there 2 weeks but in those 2 weeks, I'd seen him there almost every other day.

The other CNAs gossiped about him. They seemed to know all the info on him and didn't mind sharing it. Apparently, he was a big shot street hustler that had all the women fawning over him. I overheard them talking about his candy painted, flip flop box Chevy with the chrome rims and the speakers that you could hear from three streets over. They gushed over the fact that he walked around with a roll of money as big as their fist. They could not stop gagging over his wardrobe and noted that he was always well dressed.

His favorite was Polo. He wore nothing but the latest threads. Often, he bought the bar out at the clubs on the weekend, and all the other street niggas respected him and showed him love.

He sounded like a great catch if that was the type that you were going for. To me, those things meant nothing. I was raised in a way that fashioned me to pay more attention to someone's insides than outsides. Someone being a good person held more value to me than their possessions. I didn't have time to entertain any distractions. My goal was to work and gain experience in the medical field before taking the leap and entering nursing school. He would have to do more than be a fabulous dope boy in order to impress me.

I finished feeding Mrs. Perry, cleaned her up, and headed off to my next patient. Over the next few months, I saw Indigo every other day visiting his grandmother. I wanted no parts of the circus that seemed to surround him, so I avoided him whenever possible.

One day while out grocery shopping, I noticed that he

was on the same aisle as me. Trying to ignore him, I continued pushing my cart until I reached check out. I loaded all my groceries onto the conveyor belt, and as the cashier gave me a total, he handed me three $100 bills.

"Ummm Jordan, right? I can tell that you are independent and all, but I really want to thank you for what you do for my grandmother and how well you take care of her. All she does is complain about everyone else but never about you. You're her favorite and she really, really likes you."

The cashier smiled and blushed as if he handed it to her.

"No need to thank me. I'm just doing my job, sir. I don't want your money, but I appreciate you offering."

"It's Indigo, remember, and I'm not asking you to take it. I'm telling you to take it. Oh, and I don't take *no* for an answer. You should ask around about me."

"Trust and believe that I don't have to ask at all. You are all that they talk about at that nursing home."

"Never mind all of that. Here, girl, take this money so that we can get out of this line. We are holding people up." He flashed that gorgeous smile of his.

Reluctantly, I grabbed the money from his hand and paid the cashier. My total was only $87 so I attempted to give him the change. He refused. "Jordan, please put that in your pocket and look at it as a well-deserved tip."

Checking out with his two little items, he followed me out of the store.

"Can I help you put your groceries in the car? Oh wait, let me guess. You don't need any help with that either?"

"You're right, I don't, but I don't want to be prideful so yes, you can help me."

Walking over to my older model Honda Civic, I popped the trunk. Indigo loaded all the groceries into the car and headed back to return the buggy to the store. While he was busy trying to get back across the road, I hopped into my ride, put it in reverse, and began backing out of the parking spot.

"Wait, wait!" he yelled while running to my car. "Damn, so you are just gonna leave like that?" He said as he licked his teeth.

"I said thank you. What else am I supposed to say?"

"I just want to talk to you, Jordan. I don't bite. You are beautiful and I think that you're kind of sweet. I want to get to know you better. That's if you don't already have a man at home waiting for you."

"Indigo, or Gogo as your granny calls you, you seem like a really nice guy but I think I'll pass. I don't need two or three women at my job or coming up to my job trying to fight me about you. I've heard all of the stories."

"You mean to tell me that you don't want to talk to me based off things that you heard. None of those women at that nursing home know me personally. They only either know what they've been told or what they've made up. A couple of them have tried to get at me, but I turned them down. They don't have shit on you. It's *you* I want."

"Yeah, well that's nice to know, but I need to get home and put these groceries away. Thank you again for the money and I hope that you get home safely," I put my car back in reverse and drove out of the parking lot.

Let the Bombing Begin
INDIGO

I stood there dumbfounded, wondering how on earth I was going to get close to this angel.

I didn't know why but Jordan was all I could think about. I was determined to make her mine. After all, she was one of the most beautiful women that I'd ever seen. She stood just 5'3" with short curly blonde hair. She was the color of honey and although small in stature, she was thick in all the right places. I was intrigued from our first encounter and knew that I wanted her in my life in some capacity. I enjoyed visiting my grandmother but also enjoyed seeing her beautiful face walking the hallways.

I knew that she was dodging me but didn't care. I also knew that we would run into each other at some point in time. I promised myself that I would wait patiently until that day came. One thing was for certain, she couldn't run forever.

The women at the nursing home practically drooled when I entered the building. I heard the whispers and the side conversations. I wasn't moved by any of it because the person that I actually wanted, acted as if I didn't exist.

This made me sweat her even more. I was that nigga in this little city. I'd had my pick of the litter up until this point, I'd rarely heard the words *no* from any woman that crossed my path. That was until I attempted to step to Jordan. She spoke *no* fluently.

Jordan turning me down that day in the parking lot set off something within me. I almost became obsessed with the idea of this short sassy goddess that invaded my thoughts too frequently for me to ignore. I made up in my mind that I would stop at nothing to get close to her. I tried to pursue her every time the opportunity presented itself. Which wasn't very often. Only when I went to visit granny.

Jordan wasn't out in the streets like that, so I started bringing flowers whenever I visited the nursing home. I brought a bouquet for my granny and a bouquet for Jordan.

Although I was 9 years her senior, the sweet young thing wasn't easily swayed. Finally, after 2 months of roses every other day, nice gestures, and small gifts, I convinced her to let me take her to dinner. She agreed to accompany me if I agreed to her conditions. She wanted to pick the spot and drive her own car. I thought that it was odd but went with it. I didn't care how she got there, as long as she came.

I agreed to her terms, and she told me that she wanted to dine at the Red Lobster in town.

I laughed. "Girl, I told you that you could pick anywhere that you want to go and you choose Red Lobster? Don't you know that Red Lobster is the fast food of seafood. Why don't you let me take you to Miami so I can show you what a real seafood dinner is?"

"Indigo. If I don't feel comfortable letting you drive me to the restaurant, what makes you think that I would go out of town with you? Also, for your information, we moved a lot as a child. I've eaten at fancy places all my life. Even after all that, I still want Red Lobster, so are you taking me or not?"

"Yes, Sweets," as I began to affectionally call her. "I'll take you to Red Lobster. Meet me there tonight at 7:00 p.m.."

Once she arrived, we were seated immediately. I ordered Long Islands, a whole lobster, and the ultimate feast for the both of us.

"So, Ms. Jordan, tell me about yourself. Where are you originally from and what made you want to get into the nursing field? And please don't leave out how you ended up in Roseville."

"To start, I'm from a small town called Notasulga, Alabama. We moved around a lot due to my father's job, but Notasulga is home. My parents still live there. I moved to Roseville 6 months ago. As an incentive to work for them, Whispering Oaks Nursing Home agreed to pay my way through nursing school. I got into the field after my dad got sick. My mother hired a nurse and physical therapist to come in twice a week. I would sit back and watch the care that they poured into my daddy. With their help, he was thriving and back to normal in no time. I was simply amazed and inspired. I decided that I wanted to help nurture people back to health. That's why I do what I do."

"Now that you know a little about me, I need the deets on you, Mr. Gogo. What's your story? I'm really interested to know because your grandma is always bragging on you and your business. So, tell me, Mr. Indigo, what exactly is that business because the streets talk you know?"

"Yes, I know but they don't be talking about shit forreal. They don't know me. They just know *of* me."

"Well, let me tell you what they said. They said that you were a drug kingpin. I want to hear from the horse's mouth. No lies and don't try to bullshit me either. My mother calls me the human lie detector. I'll be able to tell if you aren't being truthful with me."

"I'll get straight to it, and I won't lie to you, Jordan. I own a couple of barbershops and a hair salon."

"Ok, so is that *all* that you do? I find it hard to believe that there are constant rumors about you being the biggest dope dealer in Roseville. Is everyone lying about that?"

Damn, she sure do ask a lot of questions. "I may have sold a little dope here and there back in the day but these days, I'm legit."

"I don't believe you. I'm telling you now, if I find out that you are lying to me, I will never speak to you again. I despise a liar. If you start out with half-truths, you will end with them and I'm not having that. Soooo, I'm going to ask you one more time and I want the truth, Indigo. Do you still sell drugs?"

She had me backed against a wall so I answered as honestly as I could. "Ok, Ok. Yes, I do but it's not on the level that you may think. I don't keep anything on me, ever. I don't keep anything where I lay my head. As a matter of fact, I don't touch any product at all. I'm at the point where I don't even have to touch the money. I've got people for all that." I stated as I nervously gulped down my Long Island iced tea.

"And you think that makes you better than the average dope dealer?" She snapped back. "I'm doing my best not to judge but I can't help it. Do you know how drugs are ruining the black community? Huh, do you?" she griped as she sat back in her chair with her arms folded.

"Wait, hold up. Jordan, you've got it all wrong. All I sell is weed. Weed isn't killing nobody." I urged, feeling judged as a muthafucka.

"Are you sure because when I heard the word *kingpin*, weed never came to mind," she lowered her brows as she sat back and took a sip from her drink. "I thought that you were some sort of crack dealer," she admitted. "Just know that I could and would never be with someone who sold cocaine nor pills in any form. I've seen what that stuff can and will do to a family and I don't want any parts of it. You shouldn't either, Indigo."

"I get what you are saying and trust me, I understand why you are saying it. We've all got that one family member. Hell, I may even have two. You don't have to worry about that much longer. I plan on getting out the game for good. I just need to make a little more money. I've got plans to open another barbershop in the next town over and then I'm out. I promise."

"Promises are nothing more than a comfort to a fool. I like you and I think that you are kinda sweet, too, but I don't want to be with a drug dealer. I'm wayyy too unstable for that. My nerves are already bad, and I would be looking over my shoulder every second of the day. Plus,

I'm trying to go into nursing. Me having a clean record is a must and I'm not about to let you or anyone else mess that up for me. I can't have any blemishes, or it could ruin my chances. I don't want to be associated with anything that could stop my progress, Indigo. I hope you understand."

"Wait... Wait, Jordan. Ok, listen, I like you a lot and whatever I have to do to make you feel comfortable, I will. Just tell me."

"I would only be comfortable with you if you stop selling drugs of any kind."

"Done!" I said before I knew it. Knowing it was a damn lie but how else was I supposed to get her on my team? I needed her and just like her, I wasn't going to let nothing get in the way of my plans.

"What do you mean *done*? You would really stop for me? You are just getting to know me, and you are telling me that you would stop it all for me? I don't believe you for one second."

"Shit, I'm serious. I think you're worth it, Jordan. Don't you?"

"I don't think I am, I *know* I am, but I didn't think that it was that easy to walk away from the game like that," she demonstrated by snapping her fingers.

"Jordan, I'm the kingpin remember. I can do what I want."

"Ok then, Indigo. Out of the game, huh? We will see."

She smiled and squeezed a lemon across her shrimp scampi.

Damn, I shouldn't have lied to her like that. I could tell that she's feeling me but if she knew that I was never leaving the game, she'd never talk to me again. So as far as she knew,. I was out the game for good. I'll worry about all that other shit later.

Dopeboy Bachelor

JORDAN

The longer we sat and talked with each other, the fonder I became of Indigo. It wasn't hard to get attached to someone like him. He was so handsome. He stood 6'3" with an athletic frame. His wavy jet-black hair was cut in a tight Caesar fade and it blended seamlessly with his thick beard. His silky smooth, dark complexion gave the strongest cocoa a run for its money and I got lost in his dark brown eyes. He possessed charisma, charm, and a silver tongue that could sell water to a drowning man. He was witty, intelligent, and the finest eye candy that I'd seen since moving to Roseville.

Indigo was hard not to like and even harder not to love. At first glance, he was the regular old run of the mill dopeboy/street nigga. It was far more to him than that. That street nigga persona was all a farce. According to

Indigo, he came from a loving two-parent household with a beautiful upbringing. His mother was a schoolteacher, and his father was a former NFL player. He graduated from high school with a 3.8 GPA and instead of going to a traditional four-year college, he decided to enter trade school to become a barber. He became one of the best in his craft and had the clientele to prove it.

Indigo was the oldest of three. He had two sisters, Uche and Armani, who he loved to life and a few nieces and nephews to boot. He was seemingly a great guy with a good head on his shoulders. Once I gave him a shot, he didn't waste any time sweeping me off my feet. Planning elaborate dates seemed to be his thing. I'd never encountered a more romantic individual. He orchestrated roof top dinners, private chefs, fancy boat trips, cruises, and so much more. He even chartered a private jet to fly to Key West to treat me to what he considered an authentic seafood dinner to be.

The first time that he made love to me was magical. He planned a romantic weekend and flew me to New York. Indigo went all out and rented the penthouse of the Roosevelt hotel. When I opened the penthouse door, the smell of fresh cut roses filled the air.

"Jordan, I know that this might look like a lot but a woman like you only deserves the best," he stated with a face full of sincerity.

"Indigo, oh my God. How did you do all of this? This is amazing," I said, shocked at the beauty of it all.

There were at least a thousand roses and hundreds of candles. Chocolate covered strawberries, champagne on ice, and six shopping bags with all designer labels were placed neatly on the bed.

"Now you know that I love roses, Indigo. You are definitely laying it on thick this weekend." I picked up a rose and put it to my nose.

"Girl, the florist in Roseville knows my name. That's how much they used to see me. I know that you love flowers just as much as I love you," he said as he nibbled on my ear. "Jordan, let me make love to you. Let me please you." Dropping to his knees, he slipped his hands under my dress. Finding my thong, he gently slid it to the side. My body trembled with excitement and anxiousness. I finally got to see what all the hype was about, and Indigo did not disappoint.

Sticking out his stiff, thick, and long tongue, he found my pleasure button and sucked my clit ever so gently. By the time he was done, his beard was thoroughly moisturized with my sweet slippery nectar. Picking me up, he carried me through the walkway of roses leading to the bed. As he laid me down, he stood up to remove his clothing. I laid there admiring the masterpiece of a man that stood before me and wondered how did I ever get so lucky.

"I know you've been waiting on this but so have I. Trust me, Indigo, it took a whole lot of strength not to jump your bones. I'm ready for this," I slid my underwear off and threw them to the floor.

I may have been young but my sexual prowess was not. I was seasoned in the lovemaking and seduction department. Not because I was super experienced but because I took the time to get to know my own body and I knew how to get what I wanted. Learning to please me first worked to my advantage. I made every sexual encounter a memorable experience.

"Come over here and make this pussy purr, Indigo, and you better not let me down either." I demanded.

Talking shit to a man of power like him, did nothing more than turn him on.

"Oh baby, don't worry. The shit that I'm about to do to you may be considered perverse in at least 15 states. I'm pulling out all the tricks for your sexy ass," he forewarned as he nestled his head between my legs. Sucking and licking my clit like a pro. He caressed my breasts and cuffed the bottom of my ass. Grabbing my waist, he pulled me to the end of the bed. He drilled my pussy relentlessly and I whimpered with satisfaction.

"My goodness, Indigo. Please don't stop. You feel so good to me. Take me, fuck me, I'm yours," I moaned as I experienced pure pleasure.

"That's right, Jordan. Talk to me, baby. I love that shit," he grunted as he quickened his stroke. I glanced up and there was a mirror mounted on the ceiling. Watching Indigo's back curve and thrust inside my sugarwalls woke up the freak in me that had been lying dormant for so long. I began fucking him back like a savage. Thrusting my pelvis against his until we both erupted like two volcanoes.

Once we were done, we laid in each other's arms, face to face, basking in the great sex afterglow. We remained like that for a short period of time before there was a knock on the door. Our dinner arrived right on time. Gold flake ribeye steaks seasoned to perfection with truffle mashed potatoes and asparagus. Indigo had this pre-planned as well.

"Indigo, you really went all out for me. I appreciate your effort and just know that it has not gone unnoticed. Your attention to detail is amazing. This must have cost you a pretty penny." I said as I admired the room, the gifts, and all the fixings.

"You let me worry about all that. This weekend was all about you. I wanted to show you how much you mean to me and how special you are. Baby, whether you know it or not, you are in a league all by yourself. These other chicks couldn't hold a candle to you. I love you, Jordan, and I want you to be mine for life."

Indigo pulled out the biggest diamond ring that I'd

ever seen. A three-carat yellow diamond engagement ring. Getting down on one knee, he grabbed my left hand and slid the rock onto my ring finger. It was a perfect fit.

"Jordan, I love you more than I ever thought that I could ever love anyone. Please do me the honor of being my wife?" he asked gleefully.

I said *yes* and a year from the date of the proposal, we were married in an elaborate wedding that sent the whole town into a tailspin. The most sought out dope boy bachelor was off the market.

I became pregnant almost immediately after we were married and our one and only child, Taji, was born. Our bundle of joy happened to be the best thing to come from this union. Besides Taji, I'd only experienced strife, betrayal, and sadness since becoming his wife. I was as unhappy as I'd ever been in my life.

Bringing my thoughts back to the present, I finished my blunt and fell into a deep sleep.

Caught Up
INDIGO

C lub Mason's was packed, and I really wasn't feeling it. After drinking all day, I was horny and ready to nail this bitch to the bed. I shot a couple of games of pool before we all dipped out. Not wasting any time, I dropped the homies off and headed straight to slim's house. I was ready to knock a bitch's socks off. I wasn't completely lying when I said that I had to drop Tick off at home. I did just that, then went back to her house and put her to sleep in the best way. It was definitely a night to remember. Now all I had to do was slip into the house without Jordan hearing. Which was a job in itself. Sweets slept as light as a feather and the softest noise woke her up. I'm not trying to start WW3 so I needed to be as quiet as possible. I looked down at my watch. It was almost five in the morning and I knew that she would act a fool if she knew what time I got home. Just as I was about to stick my key in the door, my pager went off. *Shitttt, she's up.*

Once I got in the house, I looked down at my shirt and realized that I've fucked up and I mean *bad*. There it was. A big crusty cum stain on my pants and shirt. I knew that I had to get rid of it before Jordan saw it and tried to take my head off. I mean, she's never hit me before but it's a first time for everything. Fuuuuuck..... I knew that I should have taken my clothes off while fucking that bitch, but I was just trying to get my dick wet.

I ran straight to the bathroom downstairs, grabbed a rag, and started scrubbing for my life. That's when I heard a knock at the door. *Oh, shit. I'm caught.*

Hands of Time

JORDAN

I turned over, expecting to feel the warmth of Indigo's body next to mine, but he still wasn't home. Rolling over to grab the phone, I paged his beeper and put in 911. Having to page him pissed me off even more because I bought cell phones for us both. He would purposely leave his at home and lie, saying that he forgot it. Indigo felt that it was just a way that I kept tabs on him so he would ditch it whenever possible.

It's 4:44 A.M. and I had no idea where my husband was. I slammed the phone back on the receiver and heard the front door open. I wanted to meet him at the door, but I decided to lay there and wait for him to come to bed.

Five minutes went by... no Indigo. Ten minutes passed and he still hadn't entered the room. Finally, I got up to see what he was up to. I heard water running in the downstairs bathroom. Following the sound, I knocked on the door and something drop to the floor.

"Indigo, why in the hell is the water running? What are you doing in there?"

"Umm, umm, just give me a minute. I stopped by the Waffle House after I dropped Melee off. I got syrup on my pants and I'm trying to get it out."

"You must think that I'm some kind of fool. Bring your ass out that bathroom right now before I break this fucking door down."

The water stopped running and Indigo emerged from the bathroom. I looked him up and down, looking for traces of stickiness but didn't see any. Instead, I spotted the undeniable white crusty cum stains on his pants and at the bottom of his shirt. He saw the anger in my eyes and attempted to walk past me in a hurry.

"You low down nasty, trifling muthafucka. I can't believe that you have the nerve to walk your slew footed ass up in here at 5 am with another bitch's pussy juice on you. Have you lost your mind, Indigo? I should cut your dick off and throw it in the front yard. Get the fuck out of my house now!!" I yelled.

"I'm not going anywhere, Jordan, because I haven't done anything. This is syrup like I said. What are you? The cum police or something?"

"Humph, syrup you say. If it's just syrup, then let me smell it. Bring your ass over here."

"Jordan, no, you are taking shit too far. I'm not about to let you smell my shirt or pants. You sound like a crazy woman. It's syrup like I said and that's the end of it."

"Just like I thought. You knew better. I wasn't coming anywhere near you anyway. I'm so *tired* of your shit. It's always something with you. Why don't you go back to wherever you just came from? Get the fuck out of my house and please leave as quietly as you came! I don't want Taji to wake up and hear her daddy lying to her mama for the hundredth time. You have no respect for this marriage at all. I know one thing... You and whoever that bitch is, will pay. In this life or the next. You *will* pay."

"Just what does that supposed to mean? Are you aware of something that I'm not?"

"I'm not aware of shit. I just know, what goes around comes around." I spat.

"I said that I didn't do anything, Jordan, and I meant it but if you want me to leave then I will."

"Good, leave! Take a few days' worth of clothes with you, too. I don't want to see your face for at least a week. There's no telling what I may do to you. Get the fuck out *now*, Indigo!!!!!!" I shouted as I shoved him out of my way.

Indigo trekked up the stairs to the bedroom and grabbed his Louis Vuitton duffle bag.

"You know you act ridiculous sometimes. I'm telling you to your face that I've done nothing wrong, and you still won't believe me," he muttered as he neatly folded a couple of shirts and put them in his bag. "You are supposed to be my wife and stick beside me no matter what. All I see you do is get mad and wanna argue and fight. Not tonight. I'm tired and I don't have the energy."

"I bet you don't." I griped, standing in the doorway, tapping my feet against the floor.

"You used up all your energy fucking on whatever slut you had. Indigo, don't you see by now that I'm angry and mad all the time because *you* always have some shit going on. I know that you were with somebody tonight. I'm going to find out who she is, and I promise you that the both of you will regret it."

"Everybody in this town knows we are married. We had one of the biggest weddings to ever grace this county. It's no excuse. Hell, even if she didn't know you were married, *you* do. You know Indigo, you prove to me more and more every day that I made a mistake in marrying your ass. A *big* one. I should have left you the first time that I caught you at the club with that girl sitting on your lap. I should have walked away. Then, at least I'd still have my dignity."

"Don't bring up old shit and there is nobody else, Jordan. Just you, girl. I only love you. I don't know why you are doing this but please tell Taji when she wakes up in the morning that I will be picking her up from school this week and bringing her home. That's if that's ok with you. Since you are putting me out, that will give me the chance to spend a little time with her. Anyway, I'll be at the hotel in town if you need me. I love you, Jordan, and I'm sorry that you don't trust me," he groaned as he walked past me and down the stairs.

"Don't be sorry that I don't trust you, be sorry that your sorry ass can't be trusted. Also, don't try to bring up my baby and spending time with her because you didn't care to do any of that shit before now."

I sneered as I closed my bedroom door. A few moments later, I heard the door close and immediately burst into tears. Not because of his betrayal. Sadly, I'd grown accustomed to that. I grieved the life that I could have had. This one was certainly not the life that I wanted for myself. I thought that by now I would have a successful nursing career. Several properties and businesses that we ran together. I'd always dreamed of opening my own home health care agency and maybe even a private practice for traveling nurses. Instead, I let Indigo convince me to stay home with our daughter and become a home maker. I figured that this was an ok plan because I could always go back to school. However, between raising our daughter, keeping the books for all the barbershops and salons, and attending to Indigo's needs, going back to school felt like a dream deferred.

Indigo held the purse strings. He paid every bill in the house and took care of all mine and Taji's needs. He also ran the day-to-day operations at the businesses. Even though he swore that he would stop selling drugs, he did not, he didn't even pause. He also lied about just selling weed. It wasn't until years later that I found out he was indeed selling cocaine, meth, pills, and whatever else he could get his hands on.

He was still a street pharmacist, and it made me sick to my stomach to think about it. My material needs were always met. Indigo made sure of that. I didn't want for anything. Anything except a faithful husband, quality time, attention, passion, and romance. All the things that he provided when we started our courtship. Money never mattered to me and he knew that.

Over the years, he managed to turn me into someone that I no longer recognized. Sad, needy, and insecure. Before Indigo, I was sweet and bubbly with a kind soul. People would tell me that my energy was infectious and everyone around could feel it. That was no more. Indigo was sucking the life out of me, and I didn't know how to get back to the person that I once was.

I constantly questioned myself and my intuition. He turned out to be a master manipulator and a terrible womanizer. No woman had the balls to step to me about Indigo, but I felt that it was only a matter of time before it happened. I knew that those tramps were out there, and they wanted my life. At this point, I was willing to give it to them free and clear. They had no idea what it took to walk in my shoes. I made it look good, but it wasn't easy at all.

They saw how well I was kept and wanted it for themselves. The reality of what I was dealing with made me hate the day that he walked into that room. If I could go back in time, I would have chosen a different facility.

A Dime a Dozen

INDIGO

Damn. I really had fucked up this time. I didn't know why I kept doing this shit. The look that she gave me after coming out of that bathroom almost stopped my heart. I knew that I would have to do some serious damage control to straighten this shit out.

Growing up, I saw my mother deal with the same kind of shit from my father and I hated him for it. I told myself that I would never treat my wife the way he treated my mother. I saw her stay awake crying too many nights and look at my dumb ass. Just like him. Probably worse. It was just too easy. Bitches these days didn't mind fucking up a happy home. They didn't care about wedding rings or family. All you had to do was be *that nigga* and they would jump on your dick like stank on shit.

Side pieces were a dime a dozen. Most of them didn't really want anything but a little time and attention. And I gave it to them. Knowing that I had the best thing that ever happened to me at home. I know that she didn't think it, but Jordan was the woman of my dreams. I didn't want anyone else the way that I wanted her. I didn't give a fuck about these women. I mostly fucked with them simply because I could. But my Sweets was what I lived for. I never thought it would be this easy for me to dismiss her or her feelings because I never purposely wanted to hurt her. Somehow, she always found out. It was like God made a way each time. Whether it came to her in a dream, a nosy ass neighbor, a meddling friend, or what she called, "Women's intuition." Women's intuition was a muthafucka and was never wrong from what I could see.

This time it wasn't any of that. Intuition had nothing to do with it. It was my own stupidity that got me put out and I needed to find somewhere to sleep for a few days. My first thought was to knock on Tick's door but I wasn't trying to hear that nigga's mouth. He was always preaching. "I told you so," wasn't the shit I needed at this time. A bed was, so to the hotel I went. My day was packed solid with clients. I was still a little tipsy and tired as a dog but nothing was going to stop me from getting to the money. Both ways. I needed to stop by the trap to make sure shit was shaking the way that it was supposed to, then to the barbershop to get my fade on.

I pulled into the nicest hotel that we had in Roseville. I paid for a week's stay but truly intended on being back home by this evening. Hell, they could keep it if Jordan would let me come home. Once I get in my room and get settled in, I began to really evaluate my intentions. Did I truly love Jordan or did I love *the idea* of her? Some people would tell you that if you loved someone, you wouldn't hurt them. I say that none of us were perfect. We all got hurt one way or another. She was hard to get but hadn't been hard to keep. She's kind hearted to a fault and maybe I took advantage of that. I pushed that thought to the side, along with the covers, and sleep found me before I knew it.

Like a Battle

JORDAN

H urt, tired, and disappointed was all that I was able to feel. Yet, I still had to rise to the occasion and be a mother. My heart was heavy and all I wanted to do was lie around in my sorrow but couldn't. I was raised to be strong and move with intention. My mother used to tell me that "life comes at you fast and you must be ready for anything." Those words never strayed far from my mind.

Knowing that Taji was counting on me was all the motivation that I needed. I had a regular routine and did not want to deviate from it. Every Saturday morning, I would awake before everyone else, crank the music to max volume, and began making breakfast for the family. Although it was only Taji and I that weekend, I didn't skip a beat.

I knew that Taji looked forward to her heart shaped pancakes, eggs, sausage with fresh fruit, and Welch's grape juice. I couldn't disappoint her, so I drug myself to the kitchen to get started. Grabbing my favorite CD, *The Miseducation of Lauryn Hill,* I slid it into the stereo system and let the sounds blare throughout the house.

My intentions were to drown out my own thoughts and let babygirl know that breakfast was on the way. As I allowed the music to permeate my mind, I realized that maybe I should have picked a different album. Especially considering what I was dealing with at the time. While cooking, the bass vibrated throughout my body and Lauryn spoke to my soul. I began to sway and sing at the top of my lungs.

It could all be so simple, but you'd rather make it harrrrrd. Loving you is like a battle and we both end up with scarrrrrrsss. Tell me, who I have to beeeeeee, to get some reciprocityyyyy. See no one loves you more than meeee and no one ever will.

Taji heard the music blasting and sauntered into the kitchen all crusty eyed to join me. I played the album so much that Taji knew every song and sang along with her mama.

I grabbed my daughter's hands and swayed back and forth with her while browning the sausage. Happiness was the only way to describe what I felt as I held her little hands and spun her around. I watched my babygirl throw her head back and sing like her life depended on it.

No matter how I think we grow, you always seem to let me know, it ain't workinnnnng, it ain't working... and when I try to walk away, you hurt yourself to make me stay, this is crazyyyy, oooooh, this is crazyyy.

I was so tickled with laughter that I almost burned the sausage. *These are moments to be cherished.* I thought as I looked into Taji's eyes. Minutes later, our jam session was interrupted when the music cut off. Looking up, I saw Indigo standing in the kitchen doorway.

"Shit, the party is in here." He chuckled as he pulled out a chair and sat down at the dining room table. "I made it just in time for the heart shaped pancakes. Those are my favorite, bae."

Scowling, I turned back around and began to scramble my eggs. I wanted to snap and tell him to get the fuck out, but I would never do such a thing in front of my daughter. I bit my tongue as I plated the pancakes, eggs, and sausage for Taji.

My Happy Home

INDIGO

"**D**addyyyyy," Taji yelled as she ran to embrace me. "I was wondering when you would get up. Do you have to work at the barbershop this morning?"

"Yes, I do." I said as I bopped her nose with my finger. "As soon as I'm done with breakfast, that's where I'll be headed. Why? Were you going to ask me to bring you some candy back? I know you were because you always do. You don't have to ask, my love. I'll get your *Now and Laters* and a bag of BBQ chips, ok, Taji?"

"Thank you, Daddy," she uttered as she smiled and planted a big kiss on my cheek. Shit, if no one loved me, I knew that my daughter did.

"Here you go, Sweetpea." Jordan interrupted. "We are going to continue our little dance party in a little bit, but I want you to take this tray and plate and go to your room. Stay in there until I come and get you. Go ahead and put on your cartoons and eat your breakfast. Ok, Sweetpea? Can you do that for Mommy?"

"Yes ma'am," Taji agreed as she grabbed her little tray and trekked off to her room.

"Indigo, please tell me what in the fuck you are doing here? I told you that I didn't want to see your face for at least a week. I need time away from you. Time to think!!" she fussed as she went to the other side of the kitchen. Away from me.

"Think about what? Leaving me? I hope that isn't what you are thinking about. Baby, we can work through this. I didn't do anything." I pleaded. " I'm telling you. I went and played pool for a little bit, then dropped the homey off at home. No freaky shit happened. I don't understand why you are hellbent on not believing me."

"Because you are a liar, and the truth isn't in you. You lie about everything. Even the simple shit. I can't trust anything that you say to me. I know what I saw, Indigo, and I'm not going to let you convince me that I didn't. I know what cum stains on clothes look like. I'm not a damn fool like you want to believe I am. Can you grab your pancake and *syrup* and get the fuck on out of here? Try not to spill any on your clothes this time."

That one hurt because I was indeed lying. I always lied.

A lie was just easier to tell. She would never understand the truth. My truth. I knew that it was no point in trying to get her to believe the lie that I was trying to spit so I backed out gracefully. For now at least.

"Jordan, I'm going to leave because I'm booked solid today, but this isn't over. We will talk about this later."

"You're right. Later as in next week sometime. Now please leave!!"

"Oh come on, Sweets, you don't really want me to leave, do you? If you weren't being so mean to me, I'd be making that pussy purr right now. You know you want me to," I whispered as I walked up behind her and kissed her neck.

"I have a little time before I have to be at the shop. I can make it purr now if you let me."

Scowling at me, she firmly stated. "No, Indigo. I'm not going to let you dickmatize me out of being pissed at you. You deserve all the strife that you receive from me and more. Please move from behind me and before you ask, yes, I feel your dick but no, I do not want it. There's no telling who's mouth and pussy you've had it in before you got here so you can get away from me with all that shit."

None of the shit that I was trying was working. As a last-ditch effort, I yelled, "Jordan!! I'm tired of pleading with you. I told you that I haven't done shit. That was **not** cum that you saw. I swear to you. The only reason why I was trying to get it off is because I know how you think. I knew that you would assume the worse because you always do. I didn't want you to overthink it so I decided to get rid of it before you could see it. I didn't know that you were going to come down to the bathroom. Baby, please believe me. I would never hurt you *again*. I know that I've fucked up in the past but that was a long time ago. I've learned my lesson and I've been on the straight and narrow since then. I promise, Jordan. You are the only woman that I want. You are the only one that I need, and I'd be a fool to fuck up our happy home."

"Is that what you think this is? A happy home, huh? Well, fool you are because you've been fucking it up for a while. Seriously, Indigo. You can go ahead and leave now."

"Ok, I'm leaving but I'll be back to talk about this with you later. My last client is at five o'clock, so I'll be back around that time. We have to talk about this, ok? We have to. I love you, Jordan," I mumbled as I left the house and made my rounds to take care of business.

Friend and Foe

JORDAN

I turned the CD player back on and called Taji out of her room. "Are you done eating, Sweetpea?

"Yes, Mommy, and it was good, too."

"Good, that's what Mama likes to hear. Go get your plate and tray and take it into the kitchen. Now that you are fed, you know what time it is."

"It's time to listen to music while we clean up the house." Taji responded.

"That's right. You go ahead and start with your room and be sure to dust and vacuum. You always forget that, and I'll handle the rest, ok?"

"Yes, Mommy."

"Once we are done cleaning, you and I are going to take a road trip, so I want you to bathe and get dressed. Then grab your little suitcase and pack enough clothes for an overnight stay. I want you to put 2 outfits in there, 3 pairs of underwear, and a pajama set. We are going to see Grandma and Grandpa."

I turned the sound on full blast and got to work. I cleaned the house from top to bottom. Once finished, I hopped in and out the shower and flopped down on my bed to lotion my body. As I was doing so, the phone rang.

"Hello."

"Hey, girl, I hear the music blasting. You must be cleaning up?"

"You know it, Sonia. What's up? What do you have going on today?"

"Not much but we need to talk. Not on the phone either. In person." Sonia urged.

"Well, baby girl and I were on our way out so I can stop by your house if you need me to."

"Yes, I need you to. You are going to want to hear this. I'll see you later Jordan."

Sonia hung up and I couldn't help but wonder why she needed to speak with me face to face. I didn't waste much time finding out. Once I was done getting dressed and packing my overnight bag, Taji and I were off to Sonia's house.

I pulled up at Sonia's apartment. Her nieces and nephews were running around outside playing and Taji almost jumped out of the car to join them.

"Wait, little Miss Ma'am, I didn't tell you to get out of this car yet."

"I know, Mommy, but Auntie Sonia has her sister's kids over. I want to go play with them. You know that I never have anyone to play with at home. Please let me go. I promise to be good, and I already know not to go out of the yard. I also know not to talk to strangers, Mommy. I know what I'm supposed to do. You have told me over and over. Now may I please get out and play?"

"Yes, you can. I'm going up to holler at your Aunt Sonia, but I'll be right back down. You better be here when I come back and you are not allowed to enter into anybody's house, Ok?"

I trek up the steps to Sonia's apartment. Before I could knock, the door swings open, and Sonia was standing there smoking a cigarette.

"Come on in, girl, and excuse the smell. I wanted me some chitterlings this evening, so I had to get up early and start cleaning them. They are in the crockpot now. Anyway, have a seat."

"Fuck sitting down, Sonia. What is so urgent that you have to tell me in person? I was expecting to here from Sage, not your ass."

"You don't want to hear from that bitch because I promise that she isn't a reliable source. Sage is fucking Indigo." Sonia blurted out.

"Come again? Did you say that *Sage* was fucking my husband?"

"Yep, that's exactly what I said."

"How do you know?" I could feel my body heating and starting to shake from the anger.

"Because after we left your house last night, Sage told me that after she dropped me off, she was going to go home and get ready to see her man. I didn't ask her who because she changes men like she changes her draws. Plus, she lies like a rug, so I didn't see the purpose. After dropping me off, my boo, Bane, came to pick me up and we decided to go to Mason's to have a few drinks. We went in and immediately ducked off in the VIP section up top. I peered down and there was Sage and Indigo flirting and feeling all on each other. Tick was just sitting there shaking his head. I made Bane go and get our drinks so that I wouldn't be seen and could keep on spying. I saw him with my own eyes. He grabbed her ass a few times and kissed her on the back of the neck. They left together. Now normally, I don't assume but I think that it is safe to say that they are fucking."

"Ok, I need a favor from you and don't worry, I never reveal my sources."

"Oh shit. What are you going to do, Jordan?"

I went in my pocket and pulled out the same $100 bill that Indigo had given me last night.

"Here." I licked my teeth as I handed Sonia the money. "You've been to my mama's house with me enough to remember how to get there, don't you?"

"Of course."

"I want you to take my baby to Notasulga and drop her off with my mama. I'll call her and tell her that you are on the way. I've got something to take care of."

"Jordan, I don't want you to do anything crazy. You have been talking about going to school, remember? Don't let that nigga or that bitch get you out of character."

"It's too late for all that shit, Sonia. That nigga walked in my house at 5 am this morning with pussy juice and cum stains on his pants. He's a dead man in my eyes and so is she. I'm going to kill the both of them."

"Sonia, I can't believe that Sage would betray me like that. After all that I've done for her. Old trifling ass, catfish mouth having, bad body, 27 piece wearing, milk dud head having, begging ass bitch. I gave that whore money when she was struggling. I helped feed her and her kids when she didn't have any food in her refrigerator. I even let her use my extra car a few times to get herself and those kids to work and school and she turned around and fucked my husband. Sonia, if I go to jail, please come and get me out. After stomping this bitch the way I want to, they may give me life with no parole?"

"I promise they will not get away with this. I'm about

to get my lick back in more ways than one." I sucked my teeth as I walked towards the door.

Standing in the hallway of the apartment complex, I yelled for Taji to come here. She came running.

"Hey, baby girl, come in for a minute. I know that I told you that we were going to see Grandma and Grandpa and we are, but Auntie Sonia is going to take you. I'm still coming, but I have to take care of some business first. Now I want you to be a good girl, OK. Mama loves you and I will see you later."

"OK, Mommy. Are you coming tonight?"

"Yes. As soon as I finish tying up some loose ends, I will be there."

I pulled out my cell phone to call my mother and let her know that Sonia would be bringing Taji and that I would be coming directly behind her. I didn't explain very much but just enough. I didn't need them worrying about me. After making my phone call, I hugged and kissed Taji and trekked back to my car. I fired up the engine and peeled off like I was in the Indianapolis 500.

I couldn't see anything but red and was having a difficult time trying to figure out who I wanted to fuck up first. Sage or Indigo. I decided to make a pitstop at Tick's house before confronting either of the two. I didn't care that he was Indigo's best friend. I was going to get the truth, one way or another.

Good for the Gander

TICK

Bang, **Bang, Bang.** At first, it sounded like someone was shooting at my shit so I grabbed my steel just in case. Half asleep, I realize that it was just the door. I live out in the country, away from the hustle and bustle of city life, so I was not used to passerbyers. You had to know where you were going to get to me so I was really wondering who was stopping by here without calling. Looking out the blinds, I saw Jordan standing on my porch. *What in the hell is she doing here?* Slightly cracking the door, I appeared from the shadow. She almost looked startled.

I saw her eyes glaze across my body. My morning wood was on full display, so I slid behind the door a little to give it a chance to go down. As fine as she was, I seriously doubt if that was going to happen.

Clearing her throat, she spoke. "Good morning, Tick. I don't mean to come over here and bother you, but I was wondering if I could talk to you for a minute or two?"

"Jordan, what are you doing here?"

"Did you not hear me? I just told you that I needed to talk to you."

"Does Indigo know that you are here because I don't want any shit when it comes to you?"

"Of course he doesn't but don't worry about him. He's at work and he has clients all day. Are you gonna let me in or not?"

"I'm sorry, I'm sorry, excuse my manners. Come on in. Have a seat."

I let her in and Jordan looked around at the place. I could tell that she was surprised. I wasn't the average street nigga and my place was laid. It was decorated from the top to the bottom. Glass and mirrors were my thing so they were everywhere. Along with my African sculptures and mask that I'd gotten while visiting Ghana. My walls were filled with beautiful eccentric paintings and I kept everything in perfect order. I saw her taking notes of the plasma flat screen TV. Everything in my joint had its own little place. She'd been to the spot where we handled our business a handful of times, but she'd never actually been to where I laid my head. This definitely wasn't that.

"Tick, this place is nice, and you have it decorated so beautifully. My husband must be paying you really well."

"He don't pay me shit. We earn it together." I spat.

"That's not what he says. He told me that *he* was the brains of the operation and that you were only the muscle. He led me to believe that you niggas would be lost without him."

"I mean, he does some things, but I handle most of the business. That nigga is rarely in place."

"That's not what he tells me. According to him, either he's working or he's at the spot making sure that shit runs smoothly."

"Hmmmph, that's the lie that he told you? He knows better than that. He knows that without *me*, all this shit would crumble. The connects barely know his mutha-fuckin' name." I sneered as I finger-combed my beard.

"I knew it, Tick. I knew that you were truly the man. Indigo acts like he is holding it all together but it's really you. You are really that nigga," she said as she stood up and walked towards me. Bracing herself on the couch, she slid her panties off and threw them at me.

"Yo, Jordan. What in the fuck are you doing?" I questioned because she was trying to cross a barrier that she needed not climb over.

"What does it look like? I'm getting comfortable. Besides, I'm not doing anything that you don't want me to do. Why don't you get over here and taste this pussy? You know you want to. Do you really think that I haven't noticed the way that you look at me whenever Indigo's not paying attention?"

That statement caught me off guard because I'd been real careful around her. I mean yeah, she was gorgeous so what man in his right mind wouldn't want her, but I never crossed that line. I stood there, dumbstruck, with her panties in my hands.

"Put them to your nose and take a deep breath. I want you to get a whiff of what a real bitch smells like. I'd bet good money that you've never smelled a pussy so clean." She said in a sexy, seductive tone.

"Jordan, what the fuck is happening here? Are you really trying to go there with me?"

"Well, why not? Seeing that my husband is sticking his dick in everything that moves. I figured that I may as well have a little fun for myself. I've been watching you, too, Tick, but I've kept my pussy to myself out of love and respect for him. Well, no more of that shit. I'm going to go after what I want and what I want right now is your dick down my throat and my pussy in your mouth."

"Yo, Jordan. I can't believe this shit. Please tell me that you are just fucking with me right now? Please." I begged. I wanted this to be a joke so bad but it wasn't. She had some shit on her mind. I could see it in her eyes.

"I'm serious as a heart attack, Tick. I'm not going to beg you," she said as she cocked one leg up on the coffee table.

"Does this feel like I'm fucking with you right now?" she said as she grabbed two fingers and placed it between the folds of her pussy. "Come taste me," she purred as she guided one finger inside her wet spot and she moaned seductively with delight.

I'm not going to lie. I practically fell to my knees. Jordan was short so her pussy lined up perfectly with my mouth. I went in full throttle without a second thought.

"That's it, Tick, suck this pussy." She hissed.

Grabbing the back of her ass, I pulled her closer to me and shoved her pussy in my mouth. She rocked back-and-forth, fucking my face ferociously, enjoying the stiffness of my tongue.

"Wait, Tick, wait. I don't wanna focus on standing. Let me lie down on this couch." She took a few steps back, sat down, and scooched to the end of the couch while spreading her legs. She then locked them behind her head. My eyes widened at how flexible she was. I dived back in. I sucked her pussy as if my life depended on it. Sliding a finger in, I slurped and licked until her wetness dripped from my chin and left a huge wet spot on my brand new couch.

"Yes, Tick. I see that you really know your way around

a pussy." She moaned, "I've never had head this good. That's right, daddy. Make this pussy cum." The sound of her sweet voice made me want to bust a nut immediately. I tried to think of any and everything but the fact that I was eating my best friend's wife's pussy, and it tasted phenomenal. Eventually, I said *fuck it*. It was what it was.

"Yes, Tick, yes... I'm almost there," she moaned.

I slid another finger in and pumped as fast as I could. Jordan beared down and squirted pussy juice clean across the room. A nigga was amazed. Never having a squirter before, I was more turned on than I'd ever been.

"Bring that ass here."

"Wait, Tick. Don't you want this tongue wrapped around your dick?"

"Maybe another time but right now, I want to slip and slide in this wet pussy. I've been wanting to do this for years, girl."

Grabbing her by the waist, I flipped her over and slid deep into her snatch. Jordan's back arched and she panted as I slid in and out of her wet spot. I dropped big dick in her and she didn't know how to react. I could tell that her goal was to come over and completely seduce and dominate me. Instead, I ended up giving her dick that she wouldn't be able to get off her mind. I gave her nut after nut. Something I'm sure her nigga hadn't done.

"Damn, Tick, I didn't know that you were packing all

that pipe. I should have been jumped on this dick," she said as she moaned, groaned, and fucked back.

"Shit, Jordan, you got that snapper on you. Your pussy is so tight. It feels so good around my dick." I gritted as her pussy clenched with every thrust. "OOOh, Jordan, fuck. Please stop fucking back. I don't want to cum too fast. Just stop moving. I want to savor this." I leaned down and whispered in her ear.

"That's right, daddy... slow fuck that pussy. Punish it. Deeper, Tick. Fuck me deeper."

"I want to but it's so good. You'll make me cum and I don't want to." I said through gritted teeth as I desperately tried not to finish.

I slid out of her pussy and started licking her clit from the back. My tongue was going 100 miles a minute. She bucked and shuddered as another nut was imminent. She came again and rolled over. "I want to look in your face while you're in me." She placed her legs on my shoulders and used her pelvic muscles to make her pussy talk to me.

I looked down and shook my head at how amazingly beautiful her pussy was. Sliding back in, I was taken aback by the warmth radiating from her snatch. I pulled out just enough to see her sweet pussy surrounding my thickness. I salivated at the sight of her glistening juices. She reached up and grabbed my neck. That sealed the deal for me. I loved an aggressive woman. With that, I pumped four more times and it was over. I tried to hold back but couldn't. Filling her pussy with my hotness, I grinded until I had nothing left.

Laying down beside her, I whispered, "Indigo don't know how lucky he is."

"He sure the fuck doesn't. Why do you think that I'm over here?"

She laid there smiling. The smile only lasted a second before a realization hit her. "Wait a fucking minute, Tick, please don't tell me that you nutted in me."

Yes I did and I don't know what the fuck I was thinking. "I'm sorry, Jordan, but I did. I tried to pull out. I mean, I wanted to pull out, but I just couldn't. God damn that pussy is good," I admitted as I placed my hands on top of my head. "Please don't be worried. I wear condoms faithfully. I ain't got shit and I get tested every three months so we are straight in that department. I can even show you the papers if you need me to."

"I believe you, Tick. You look like the kind of nigga that takes care of himself so I'm not tripping. It should be all good because I take that pill like clockwork. Where is your bathroom? I need to go clean up."

"Follow me, I'll show you. The washrags and towels are in the linen closet behind the door. There is some Dove soap in there, too," I advised as Jordan followed me down the hallway.

I motioned to the left, showing her the restroom. "Thank you, Shug," she chirped as she kissed me on the lips and closed the bathroom door. "I'll be right out."

I stood by the door still in disbelief. Not being able to digest what just happened. An unfamiliar feeling started to come over me and it wasn't guilt but a strong desire to shield her from the bullshit that came with Indigo. I knew that she was too good for him but my loyalty to Indigo wouldn't let me step to her in the past. Diving inside that sweet pussy of hers gave me a change of heart..

Damn, her pussy juices must have magic in it because I think I'm in love.

"Jordan," I yelled through the bathroom door. "You should have never let me taste that sweet thang. I don't know if I can ever get it out my mind, girl. What did you put in that stuff?" I laughed while smelling my top lip.

Jordan emerged from the bathroom. Looking refreshed and beautiful like she always did.

"Now Tick, I know that I don't need to tell you that this stays between you and me. You are a smart man, so I don't need to say that do I?"

"Nawl, Jordan. I got you. My lips are sealed."

"That's great when it comes to what just happened between us. But I need them bitches to be wide open when it comes to telling me what I need to know. I need you to tell me what the fuck is really going on. Is my husband fucking a bitch in the Saxton projects?"

"Jordan, I'm not trying to get in—"I stopped talking and flashed a quaint little smile.

"Stop it with that loyalty shit," she commanded. "That nigga doesn't have loyalty to anyone but himself. He don't give a fuck about you or me. You are stupid to think that if he had the chance to fuck on your bad bitch, that he wouldn't because he most definitely would. Since you don't want to answer that question, maybe you'll answer this one. Is he fucking Sage?" she questioned, cutting her eyes at me.

Putting my head down, I cuffed my chin and tried not to look into Jordan's eyes.

"Shit, Tick, there is my answer right there. The look on your face tells it all. How long, Tick?"

"About two years."

"Two muthafucking years! You have got to be shitting me. This bitch has been smiling in my face and fucking my husband behind my back for two years. Oh, this bitch has got to get hers and he is already getting his."

"Honestly, Jordan, I've told Indigo over and over that he shouldn't do you like that, but that nigga never listens. I told him just last night that he was flaw but he shook that shit off and kept on pushing. I scold him every time I see him doing fucked up shit but he's a grown man. I can't make him respect you. I'm sorry, Jordan. You definitely deserve better."

"Indigo will always be my nigga, even if he doesn't get any bigger, but I've never liked the way he moved when it came to you. I've asked him countless times why he got married if he was going to still be out here in these streets chasing these bitches. The only answer I've ever gotten was, "Jordan is mine and no other nigga will ever have her like I have her. I had to hurry up and take her off the market."

"He's such a selfish son of a bitch but it's ok. I've got something for that ass. Please don't worry, Tick. He will never find out that this happened. I don't want you to have a hostile work environment," she giggled.

"This will be our little secret. I love the way that you dove in this pussy. If we are being honest with each other, I only came over to get revenge. Now that I see how good it is, I'm thinking that we should do this more often. Hell, if he can have a side, so can I, but we will have to play this thing cool. Don't change up. Still be who you are."

"You think that I'm slow or something don't you, Jordan? I knew *exactly* why you were doing what you were doing. You weren't fooling me, girl. I would have said and done anything that you asked me to. Truthfully, he deserves whatever you do to him. I see how that nigga really gets down. You only got a sliver. He is real deal grimy as fuck so I'm glad that you are getting a little get back. I'm even happier that you chose me to do it with. I've been warning this nigga for years that he better start treating you right. He didn't listen so it is what it is."

"I want you to know that you have made my day. That was the best dick that I've had in ages. And if you're wondering, you have no competition. Please know that. I was just talking shit earlier when I said that you were the man, but yeah, you really *are* that nigga," she said as she sauntered to the front door.

I smiled at her, kissed her softly, slapped her on her ass, and saw her out.

Home Sweet Home

JORDAN

Racing down the highway, I cut in and out of traffic until I arrived at Sage's apartment complex. I noticed that her car wasn't in its usual spot, but I knocked on the door anyway. Her oldest daughter answered.

"Hey, lil mama, is Sage here?"

"Yeah, Ms. Jordan, she's back there asleep. Do you want me to wake her up?"

"Ummm, are your brothers and sisters here?"

"Yes, they are both in the bed with her."

"Oh, ok then. In that case, don't wake her up. Just tell her that I came by and that I will catch up with her later."

"Ok, Ms. Jordan. I will."

I badly wanted to confront Sage but I wasn't willing to traumatize the children in the process. I wouldn't want anyone bringing strife to my home so instead, I left and went on about my way.

I got on the highway heading towards my hometown. Notasulga, Alabama. I tried to come up with something to explain my impromptu visit, but I hated to lie to my parents. I decided that I would tell them just enough to let them know that there was a problem but not enough for them to be truly concerned. I arrived just as the sun was descending, and nightfall was breaking through. Once I arrived, Taji met me at the door with open arms.

I entered and the smell of cornbread dressing and cabbage filled the air.

"Mama, don't tell me that you are making dressing. You know it's my favorite," I said as I handed Taji her tiny suitcase and placed mine in the corner.

"Well, I won't tell you then," my mama chirped as she grabbed me and hugged me tightly.

"Where is Daddy?"

"Child, John is somewhere around here. Probably out back in that garden watering those plants. You know it's springtime and your daddy doesn't play when it comes to his vegetables."

"Is there anything that I can do to help in the kitchen?"

"No, Jordan, my grandbaby and I have it all covered.

Taji, why don't you go out back with your grandpa for a little bit and let me have a talk with your mother."

I pulled out a chair from the kitchen table and braced myself for the questions.

"Now you know, I'm not the one to get in your business because you are grown, but I'm your mama and I know when something's not right."

"It's really not a big deal, Mama. I'm a little upset at Indigo right now, but I'll be OK. I just wanted to get away for a day or so and come and check on you and Daddy. Is something so wrong with me coming home?"

"Not at all. I love when you come in, but you usually don't drop in like this. I'm not gonna ask you any more questions or try to get in your business because if you want me to know, you'll tell me. I know you didn't ask for this advice, but I'm gonna give it to you anyway. Marriage has a whole lot of ups and downs. There are gonna be some days that you love the ground that he walks on and other days, you are gonna want to run him over with your car. Remember that on both days he's your husband and when you got married, you became one."

"Well, I sure as fuck wish someone would have told him that," I mumbled to myself.

"Excuse me, young lady. I heard that!"

"I'm sorry, Mama. I was just thinking out loud. I heard you. I heard every word."

"Now go over there in that pantry and pull out those teabags and make us some iced tea. We're going to eat good tonight."

"Sassy, I believe that a gopher or a damn armadillo or something is digging up our backyard." John laments as he burst through the back door. "Oh, hey Jo, come over here and give your daddy a hug. I didn't know you were going to be here this soon. It's good to see you, baby."

"It's good to see you, too, Daddy."

"Little Taji makes a great helper in the garden. She listens very well and learns even quicker. Maybe I'll come up there to Roseville and help y'all plant a garden."

"Daddy, I don't have time for a garden. I'm about to go to school."

"Well, it's about damn time. I was wondering when you were gonna make that move. What does your husband have to say about that?"

"Shut up, John, and stay out of her business. You are so damn nosy." Sassy fussed.

"I'm not being nosy, Sassy, I'm just saying. She was supposed to go down there to Roseville to further her education. Instead, she got caught up with that Indigo and ain't said shit else about nursing in years. So, I can't lie. I'm glad that you are doing what you said that you were going to do. You have me and your mama's full support. The real question is when do you start?"

"Not sure yet, Daddy. I haven't started the paperwork yet, but it will be soon."

"When you start, I want to be the first to know. I'm going to buy you your very first pair of ugly nursing shoes," he snickered.

Giggling right along with him, I responded, "I appreciate that, Daddy. Now, how long before we get to eat? I haven't had a bite since this morning, and I am starving."

"I'm just waiting for the dressing to brown and we will be ready. The chicken is already done and so is the fried cabbage, the candy yams, and the macaroni and cheese."

"Mama, all of that sounds so good. I can't wait. I'm going to go into my room and slip on something more comfortable, and I'll be right back out. Hopefully, by that time, everything will be ready, and we can grub." I grabbed my bag and sashayed to my bedroom.

Moments after I entered the bedroom, my cell phone rang, showing a call from my house. Ignoring it, I threw the suitcase on the bed and pulled out my favorite mumu and a pair of slippers. The phone stopped ringing briefly and then began ringing again.

Sweets Gone Sour

INDIGO

I came home to an empty house. I guess I should be happy to see that all the furniture was still here but my wife and child were gone. Shit like that I couldn't tolerate. I told her that I would be back after work. Sweets wanted all the smoke I see. Picking up the phone, I called her cell. She didn't answer. So I called back and this time, she answered.

"What do you want, Indigo?" she hastily asked.

"I want to know where the fuck my wife and kid is. I told you that I would be back over here when I got off, so where are you?"

"I knew you wouldn't stay away, so I decided to go away for a minute. Don't worry about where I am. You refuse to respect my wishes. I said to you this morning over and over that I didn't want to talk to you or see you for at least a week and you won't even wait a day."

"Jordan, I shouldn't have to wait a second. What kind of wife runs away from her husband?" I scolded.

"What kind of husband goes out and stays out all night and comes home with another bitch's bodily fluids on him? Since we are asking questions, answer that one." She fired back.

Well damn. Sweets ain't so sweet today. More like sour.

"I did, Jordan, and you don't believe me so I'm not answering it again. When the fuck are you coming back home? You know what, nevermind. You don't even have to answer that because it doesn't matter. I brought all of my shit back to the house anyway. Just know that when you get back, I'll be here. We are married and I'm not going nowhere. We are one and you shouldn't run away when you get pissed."

"My mother told me that same stupid shit. One my ass. More like we are three, four, or five," she retorted.

Confused, I asked, "Three, four, or five? What does that mean, Jordan? What are you talking about?"

"Never mind. You won't admit to it anyway. I've got to go," she urged before hanging up in my face.

There were several ways to piss me off and one of the top five was to hang up in my face. That shit was so disrespectful.

Fuck this. Since she wanted to play and not tell me where she was, I guess I would play, too. I'd slide through and see Slim for a minute. I bet that she had time for me. I don't understand women. They wanted you to do right and when you try, they got mad and left. What kind of shit was this?

Leaving the house, I hopped in my ride and headed across town. Stopping at my favorite liquor store, I picked up a bottle of that white Christian brothers. I was in the mood for something smooth. Alcohol had a way of helping me take my mind off my reality. My life was a little fucked up but it could always be worse I guest. I needed to call my boy Tick. I hadn't heard from him today but maybe that's not a bad thing. No news was good news.

Imani was happy as fuck when I slid through. She came outside to meet me and sucked my dick right there in the parking lot. She brought that sweet mouth straight to me. The day may have started out rough but it may just end up alright. The night was still young and I wanted to see where it took me.

Malnourished

JORDAN

Arguing was never my thing. I'd walk away before I let someone take me there but Indigo had a way of bringing out the worse in me these days. I regrouped and took a couple of deep breaths to calm down. I opened my bedroom door and entered back into the room where my parents were setting the table and assembling plates.

I pushed the conversation with Indigo to the back of my mind and tried to enjoy a quiet evening with my daughter and parents. After everyone was stuffed, I put Taji to bed and went out back on the screened in porch. I loved to listen to the sounds of the night wind rustling, along with the crickets and frogs. I watched the lightning bugs illuminate the garden, something that I often did as a child.

I reflected over how much time I'd wasted with Indigo and knew that things would never be like they used to be. He'd done too much damage to the relationship and didn't appear to want even remotely to change his ways. I wanted to stay for baby girl's sake but realized that staying in a terrible marriage for the sake of children, hardly ever ended up well. In the end, the children suffered more and often in silence. I didn't want that for my daughter but didn't know where to begin.

I gotta figure this shit out because I can't keep doing this.

The next morning before daybreak, my cell phone rang again.

A drunken voice muttered, "I can't believe that you didn't come home. Where are you, Sweets? Where is my baby? I miss you. I miss you so much. I'm sorry, I'm sorry for everything. I don't know why I do the shit that I do. But I know that I don't wanna do it anymore."

"Indigo, stop. Just please... stop because you don't mean anything that you're saying. You are drunk and you need to take your drunk ass to bed." I ordered.

"I'm serious, Jordan. Please listen to me. I'm gonna do everything that I said I was going to do. I'm going to get out the game for real this time. Tick and Melee can have this shit. I'm ready to be the husband that you need."

"Is that so? Now that I'm pissed, you're all of a sudden

ready to be the man that I need. How typical of you, Indigo."

"I'm wrong, I know that I'm wrong and I don't have any excuses. Only accountability. I'm fucked up about you. I'm for real, Jordan. I need you. Coming home to this empty house just doesn't feel right. It ain't right. Please come home."

I listened quietly, hanging on to every word until he became silent. I waited a few seconds before responding. "I hear what you are saying but what makes this time any different from the last or the time before that or the time before that? I keep on forgiving you and you keep on doing the same shit to me. You constantly lie to me, you bait me with false promises, you don't spend any time with our daughter. I'm tired. I don't know how much more of this shit I can take."

"I'm sorry. Please don't say that, baby. I know you are tired, but I swear that I'm going to change. Just please don't leave me. I won't make it if you do. I'd find the tallest bridge that I could and jump. That's how much you mean to me, Jordan. I can't do this life without you and I don't want to. Please tell me that you forgive me. If you forgive me this one time, I won't make you regret it. I'm gonna do right by you and Taji. I am nothing if you are not by my side."

"We will see," I whispered as I hung up the phone.

He really did sound sincere this time. Maybe he will be different. I've never left home before. Maybe me leaving made him look at things from a different perspective. I do love his ass. I just don't like his ways. I looked over at my baby girl, resting peacefully.

She deserves a father. What kind of person would I be to take her away from him? Feeling conflicted, confused and trapped, I dozed off and went back to sleep.

My father systematically got up at sunrise every morning to water his garden. He stopped at my door, lightly tapping to wake me.

"Jo, are you asleep?"

"Not anymore, Daddy. What's up?"

"Throw your house coat on and come out back with me. I need to talk to you for a moment."

Kissing Taji on the cheek, I slipped my house shoes on and trekked out back at my father's request.

Pointing at the tomato plants, he handed me the garden hose and directed me to start watering. He grabbed a lawn chair and had a seat while I did as I was told.

"Jo, do you know why I love gardening so much?"

"No, Daddy, why?"

"Because I've done the research to make sure that whatever I put in this ground gives me a bountiful harvest. God has given us the seeds, but he did not send down explicit instructions on how to care and grow each different plant. You have to figure that out on your own through trial and error. Some plants you can't plant together. Some do well with flowers mixed in between them. Growing something comes with a lot of responsibility. It's so much more than throwing a seed in the ground."

"Daddy, I re——-,"

"Hush, girl," he said, cutting me off mid-sentence. "I'm trying to explain something to you. Now, yes, if you plant that seed, it's going to most likely start sprouting, but if you don't nurture it properly, it will shrivel up and die."

"Daddy, what are you trying to tell me? You are just talking in riddles. Say what you want to say to me."

"Well, I don't wanna say too much because I don't need your mama fussing at me for getting in your business, but baby girl, I was not born last night. When you walked in this house, your face was as long as the day. I don't need to know what's going on, but what I am telling you is that if you are not getting watered and nurtured the way that you need to be, you will remain a tiny little seedling. No matter how healthy the seed is, if the environment isn't right, that seed will perish. In short, if you need to come home, come home."

"I would never tell you to leave your husband because that is truly your business, darling. However, being your father, I need you to know that you don't have to stay anywhere that you don't want to be. Notasulga isn't going anywhere, and neither are we and that's all I'm gonna say about that. Now, make sure you put a lot of water on those squash because squash need tons of water to grow and don't forget those zucchinis to your left."

"Yes, Daddy," I said as I marinated on my father's words.

"Now, you can go on back in that house before your mama comes out here and sees you. She's going to swear I held a gun to your head and made you water this garden."

"Dad, if we're being honest, you didn't give me much of a choice, but I'll keep that secret between you and me." We chuckled.

I smiled as I handed him the hose and went back into the house. I climbed in the bed with my daughter and attempted to lie back down, but my spirit was unsettled. Indigo's voice played over and over in my mind and so did the image of Tick's stiff tongue sliding across my clit. I got wet just thinking about him.

Wait wait wait. All of this is too much to digest. I really need to get my shit together.

About an hour later, my mother arose and started

whipping up breakfast. Taji and I enjoyed our breakfast, bathe, and got dressed. I packed up our things and said our goodbyes before getting back on the road heading to Roseville.

Inside the Lines

INDIGO

I woke up with the worse hangover that I'd ever had. I guess that was what I get for cutting up the way I did last night. I was so fucked up that driving home wasn't possible. I would have probably killed myself and someone else if I did. I ended up calling Tick to come scoop me and bring me home. I can't lie, coming home to an empty house in the middle of the night felt wrong and I knew that it was all my fault. I had to find a way to get her to come back home so I tucked my head between my legs, put my pride to the side, and begged her like Keith Sweat did.

I laid it on thick as possible and while I'm not for sure, I hoped that she felt where a nigga was coming from. I hoped that she would see that I meant her no harm and that she needed to bring her ass home. My daughter deserved to sleep in her own bed in her own room. I knew that she needed to cool off. I promised myself that I wouldn't worry unless she wasn't home by nightfall. I can't blame her for being pissed but she loved me, and I knew that she would forgive me. She always did.

The one thing that I loved about women was that they had tender hearts. I was a man and men are going to fuck up. That's just a fact of life. If women were going to be with us, they would have to love us through the bullshit sometimes. I'd put Jordan through a lot in the past couple of years and I hope that I hadn't pushed her to the edge.

I got up and paced the floor for hours. Waiting to hear from her again. Hearing Jordan's car idle in the front yard made my heart skip a beat. Finally, my baby was home.

I opened the car door and greeted them. "Man, you two just don't know how happy I am to see your beautiful faces. Come over here, baby girl, and give your daddy a hug. I could sure as hell use it. Your mama done scared the shit out of me." I said, fixing my eyes on Jordan.

"How, Daddy? How did she scare you?" babygirl asked.

"Oh, baby, don't mind me. Daddy is just kidding around. She didn't really scare me. I knew you both would be back home soon," I gabbed, setting my eyes on Jordan.

"Come give your husband a hug. Aren't you happy to see me, too?" I asked.

"Of course she is, Daddy," Taji said cheerfully. "Mommy, come hug Daddy."

I could tell that she didn't want to disappoint Taji, so she drug herself over to me and grabbed me around the neck. I embraced her tightly as we walked into the house.

"Yes, husband. I'm happy to see you, too," she chimed as she flopped down on the couch.

"It's Sunday family. What are we going to do today?" I questioned. "I was thinking that since it's still early, we could put on our Sunday's best and check out that church that you've been talking about."

Jordan's head snapped around like she was possessed. "So, you are telling me that you want to go to church?"

"I wanna go wherever you wanna go, Jordan," I advised.

"I'm a little tired this morning, but maybe next week. Let's see if you still have the same glimmer in your eye for church." Rolling her eyes and pushing me to the side, she addressed Taji.

"Baby girl, can you drag your suitcase into your room and unpack, please. Your father and I are going to go out back and have a conversation, OK?"

Taji nodded her head *yes* as she skipped out of the room.

Jordan began to walk out on the patio and turned to

see if I was behind her. "Hurry up, slowpoke, because we've got some things to discuss," she teased.

"I'm coming, girl, just give me a minute," I grunted as I hoisted myself off the couch.

Sitting down in the patio chair, Jordan crossed her legs and started in. I knew that this talk was coming and I was willing to do whatever she asked of me to make it right.

"First, I want you to understand that the only reason why I came back as quickly as I did, is because of our daughter. You said a lot of things on the phone last night and I don't even know if you remember half of them, but I don't want any miscommunication, so I want to make things clear."

"I am sick and tired of your lies. I am sick and tired of the way that you treat me, and I will not stand for it any longer. If you don't get your shit together and I mean quickly, then you can consider us **done**. I'm not doing this back-and-forth with you anymore, Indigo. I am truly *exhausted*."

"Any smidgen of trust that I had in you is gone and it is your responsibility to gain it back. I need to see change and not just for a week either. Nothing will be given to you anymore. All the shit that I once gave to you and you took advantage of will have to be earned. That goes for everything... my affection, my love, my trust. Things that I gave freely, will now come at a cost."

"I know you and I know that you have a habit of back-sliding," she said. "Understand the minute that I see you coloring outside of the lines is the minute that I will leave your ass high and dry."

"Damn, Jordan, it's like that? I guess you're not playing with the OG then. Like I said last night, I know I fucked up and I'll do whatever it takes to make it right. I'm going to stay in the house more, quit going to the clubs, and all that other shit."

"I hear you talking, Indigo, but you're gonna have to come with more than words."

I could tell that she was dead serious. There wasn't a smile or smirk in sight. I tried to ease the tension by saying, "You know I've got more than words," I said as I stroked the bulge in my pants. "You know you being all aggressive with me and telling me what I will and won't do, makes me horny as fuck. What do you say we go upstairs and make some shit shake?" I asked with a slick grin. She fired back with a headshot.

"I think you just misunderstood what I said. Everything that I gave freely will now have to be *earned* and that includes the slit in my pussy. I have no desire to fuck you right now. If you want some of my pussy, then you've got to work to change that."

"Damn, Jordan. Are you serious?" I huffed.

"Yes, I'm serious because I know something that you don't think that I know."

"And what's that?" I whispered while reaching over to rub her thigh.

She pulled back. "That you and Sage are fucking. Please don't try to deny it because I know for a fact that you are. You've been fucking for about two years. I'm not gonna sit here and scold you about it because to be honest, I don't have the energy. What I will tell you is that she is a slut and has been since the day that I met her. She's been with just about everybody on her block so before you can climb back into my walls, you have to go get tested."

I lowered my head before looking up at her with guilty eyes. I could feel the blood draining from my face. I didn't know how she knew but she did. How in the fuck did she always find out? May as well confess. I didn't have shit to lose at this point. "Like you said, Jordan, there is no need for me to lie. I was dealing with her for a little minute, but I swear to you that it is over. You know I hate doctors, but I will go get tested if you want me to."

"Oh, that wasn't me asking. That was me *telling*. I've given all of my demands. Do you have any?"

"Yes, Jordan, just one. Please don't leave me. That's my only demand. You are damn near perfect, bae. I wouldn't change a thing about you and our life. It's me that was fucked up. Never you." I confessed.

"I can't promise you anything, but I have to admit that it feels so good to hear and see you take accountability. I appreciate that you are willing to admit to your wrongdoings. I like this side of you, and I hope this side of Indigo sticks around for good. I don't want you to be perfect. I just want you to be better." She then got up from her chair, rubbed the back of my neck, and returned back into the house.

Tick Tick Boom

As I entered back into the house, I saw Taji in the kitchen making herself a peanut butter and jelly sandwich.

"Mommy, I was just about to come out there and get you. The phone rang and I answered it. It's Auntie Sonia and she wants to talk to you."

"Thank you, baby," I chirped as I picked up the phone from the countertop.

"What's up, girl?"

"Jordan, is your man around you?"

"Not at the moment. He's out back on the patio marinating on the conversation I just had with him. What's up?"

"Sage called me this morning and said that you came by her place yesterday, but she was asleep. She wanted to know why you stopped by and I didn't know what to say to her."

"Ummm, Taji, can you please take your sandwich in the livingroom and eat it, baby? Get a paper towel and be sure not to get any of that jelly on my carpet."

I waited for Taji to leave before answering Sonia's question.

"Oh, that's easy, just tell her that I know what's been going on and when I see her in the streets, I'm going to stomp a mudhole in her ass. It doesn't matter how or when, she's going to get this beat down. It's bad enough that she fucked my husband, but she sat in my face, ate my food, drank my liquor, played with my daughter, and used me. Oh yeah. She's getting tapped. That's the real reason for the ass whooping."

"I understand, Jordan. What I want to know is if you confronted Indigo as well? You can't have that energy for her and let him off scot free," she advised.

"Yes, I did. He knows that I know and admitted to it."

"Oh wow, Jordan. So, are you going to try to work through it with him?"

"I don't even know how to answer that, Sonia. I don't know what we're doing. He says that he's changing and that he's going to do better, but as you know, I don't trust him as far as I can throw him. To be honest, me telling him that we could work it out was just basically buying me more time to get my shit together. He's going to fuck up because he doesn't know how to do anything else. This time when he does, I'm going to bounce. I don't have any more fight left in me."

"I know that's right. You know men like that rarely change; they just become better at lying. A nigga like Indigo isn't going to go down without a fight. I don't think it will be as easy as you think to get away from somebody like him. Especially with how he moves."

"Well, he won't have a choice, now will he?"

"I hope you know what you are doing, Jordan. Just know that I'm rocking with you and if you need me, just give me a call."

"You know I will. I love you, Sonia."

"I love you, too, Jordan."

Indigo came back in from outside, stretched, and grabbed a glass from the cabinet.

"Who were you on the phone with, baby?" he queried as he poured cranberry juice into his glass.

"That was Sonia. She was just trying to see if I made it back."

"OK, well, I didn't get much sleep last night so I'm gonna go upstairs and take a nap. I'm still tired as hell. When I get up from my nap, I'm going to swing through Tick's place to pick up some keys. Is that OK with you?"

"You don't need permission from me. You are a grown

man, and you know right from wrong. Like I said, if you stay in the lines, we are good." I said as I grabbed my car keys.

"I'm going to take Taji to the park while you're sleeping. We'll be back in a couple of hours."

I put a few snacks in a small lunch bag and Taji and I headed to the park. While Taji swung from the monkey bars, I spotted Tick riding through the parking lot. He parked and raised his motor. He didn't get out. Instead, he rolled his window down and whistled for me to come to the car.

Jogging, I sped to his passenger window. "What are you doing here, Tick?"

"I was leaving one of my homeboy's houses and saw your car parked in the parking lot. How are you and most importantly, how's my girl doing?"

"I'm doing good and she's over there on the monkey bars having the time of her life."

"Good to know, but I know that Taji is good. I was asking about fat mama between your legs," he chuckled.

I cracked up laughing. "Tick, you are so crazy. I can't lie. I've been thinking about you too ever since that day. It's like I can't get it out of my mind," I confessed as I blushed and twirled the soft curls of my hair.

"Girl, you just don't know. You're so motherfucking sexy to me. I would give my left leg to have a woman like you by my side. There aren't many women out here that compare to you. Trust me, I know. I'm in the streets every day and the women are getting more scandalous as the years go by. I may hustle and everything, but I'm a bit old-fashioned when it comes to the type of women that I like and I love your style. You are loving, caring and so sweet, Jordan," he said while flashing his beautiful smile at me. "You take care of your daughter and Indigo like it's second nature. I'm not gonna lie. It makes me feel some kind of way to see you take such good care of a nigga that doesn't appreciate or deserve it."

"No, he doesn't but he says that he's trying so we will see."

"When did this trying start? Because he had me pick him up from Sage's house about 4 o'clock this morning. He was pissy drunk so I'm guessing that they had a good time."

"Wowwwww. This nigga really doesn't have any shame. He called me crying this morning. It had to be right after you dropped him off from being with that bitch. You know what's sad? It's sad that it doesn't surprise me at all, Tick. I'm not even mad. I'm so over this relation-ship, but I can't run away from it just yet. I'm getting my ducks in a row. I've got to plan this thing out to the max. For now, *I'm just going to sit back and see what the wall looks like,* like Miss Ceily said. If you see him on that fuck shit again, I need you to find some way to let me know. Deal?"

"Bet, Lil Mama." Tick affirmed.

"Tick, I want you to take down my cell number. Text me if anything pops off."

Telling him my number, he writes it on a receipt that he found in the console. Then he reached in his pocket and pulled out five hundred dollars in cash and handed it to me.

"Here, Sunday dinner is on me. I want you to take this. You and baby girl go to the mall and get yourselves something nice and then I want you two to have a nice dinner. On me. Don't buy Indigo shit with my money either. Let his ass eat sandwiches or something," he said jokingly.

"That may not be a bad idea. After knowing that he was out fucking on that bitch this morning, I may make that nigga eat concrete." I retorted. "But anyway, I'm not pressed anymore with what and who he does. He's not doing me, that's all I know."

"And how sad that is for him," Tick murmured with a smile.

"Thank you for the dough, Tick, but I've got to go and get back to Taji."

Tick chunked up the deuces and peeled off. I switched back towards the bench where I was sitting. Aware of the moistness forming between my legs, I smiled as I held the wad of cash in my hand. I couldn't help but think of what a nice gesture that was.

I definitely picked the wrong friend. I should've met his ass first.

A for Effort

INDIGO

fter waking up from my nap, I realized that I needed to do something to shock her, so I got up and started dinner while she was gone. Cooking was not my ministry but today, I was going to get in that kitchen and make some shit shake for my family. I needed to show her that I was serious. This was a start. She needed to see that I was here for her and my babygirl and that I would do anything to fix this. I went to the freezer to see what we had in there to thaw out and cook. I decided on meatloaf and mashed potatoes. She loved meatloaf but I knew that she would appreciate the effort more than anything.

I did what my I'd saw my mother do when I was a kid. I got the ground meat, threw some seasonings in it, and put in it the oven. Twenty-five minutes in, smoke clouded the kitchen and had me in a chokehold. I saw Jordan pull up through the window and was happy that she came home when she did. Hopefully, she would be able to save this meal.

She walked through the door with a look of disgust on her face. Like damn, I thought that she would be happy that I was trying but she had her nose in the air and a scowl was etched across her face.

"What's wrong with you, girl?" I asked.

"Indigo, what are you doing? What is that smell?" she frowned as she held her nose.

"Oh shit, baby. I may need your help. I was in here trying to make meatloaf with mashed potatoes for Sunday dinner, but it's not going too good. We may have to go out to eat because I think I have fucked this up." I laughed.

"It damn sure looks like you have, but I appreciate the sentiment. I can't remember the last time that you were in this kitchen calling yourself cooking. It had to be at least five years ago."

"I'm just trying to show you that I'm serious. I wanna put that smile back on your face. Don't think I haven't noticed that you're unhappy. Believe it or not, it hurts me to know that I'm responsible for that." I said as I lowered my eyes.

Ignoring my statement, she offered. "Why don't we

just order takeout or something and you can go pick it up?"

"That's not a bad idea at all. I have to go get these keys anyway, so I'll pick it up on my way back in."

Jordan placed the order, and I promptly left to go handle business.

The Final Straw

JORDAN

While Indigo was gone, there was a knock at the door. I peeked through the blinds and saw two men that I didn't recognize. Cracking the door just a smidge, I stood behind it. "Umm, yes. How may I help you?" I said with a smile.

"We are looking for Indigo," they uttered in unison, looking like two mean ass rattlesnakes.

"I'm sorry, but he's not here. Should I tell him who came by?"

"Tell him that the Juarez brothers are looking for him. Tell him that he's got till the end of the week to take care of us. He should know what we are talking about," one of them said as they stepped away from the door and returned to their car.

Who the fuck were they?

Nervously, I called Indigo's cell phone. As usual, he didn't answer so I paged him 911. I waited a few minutes for him to call me back and when he didn't, I called Tick's number.

The phone seemed to ring for an eternity and just as I was about to hang up, he answered.

"Are you trying to get both of us murked? The nigga was just about to leave when you called. What's up?"

"Is he gone already?" I asked nervously.

"Yeah, he just left. What's wrong?"

"Two Mexican dudes just pulled up to the house asking for him. Tick, who the fuck are they and what do they want?"

"Did they say what their names were?"

"Yes, they said that they were the Juarez brothers and that he had a week to get them their shit. What in the fuck is going on?"

"I honestly don't know, Jordan. I didn't know he had any business with them. I told him a long time ago not to fuck with them. They are grimy and they don't even like black people to be honest."

"There is no telling what this son of a bitch has gotten himself into. Whatever it is, he needs to fix it because I don't need anyone pulling up at my shit questioning me. Especially with my baby girl being here." I grumbled.

"I know what you mean, Jordan. Anyway, you've got my number. Call me if you need my help with anything."

"OK, Tick. Thanks, and I will talk to you later, bye."

Hanging up, I began to tremble at the thought of what was to come. Less than 24 hours ago, Indigo told me that he was getting out of the game and now two random men were showing up on my doorstep.

To take my mind off things, I began to get Taji ready for bed. I ran her bath water, picked her clothes out for school the next day, and styled her long beautiful tresses.

Indigo trekked through the door, jovially. I sent Taji to her room so that I could privately discussed what happened while he was away.

"Indigo, who in the fuck are the Juarez brothers? They came by here looking for you."

"They came by here? What did they say?"

"They said that you had till the end of the week to get them their shit. How are you going to tell me that you are getting out the game and you've got some Mexican niggas pulling up at our house? You know I don't play that shit. I don't even like when your homeboys come over here, so you know that I'm heated."

"It's nothing, baby, don't worry about it. I'll take care of it."

"Please do because I'm not about to be scared in my

own home. You need to get rid of them and I mean for good."

"Fuck, Jordan!!!" he yelled. "I just said don't worry, damn!! Let me handle my motherfucking business!!"

"Wait a damn minute. Who in the fuck do you think you are talking to like that? Don't you **ever** raise your voice at me that way again. I'm not the motherfucker looking for you. *They* are. Be mad at them, not me. Hell, be mad at yourself for getting into whatever you did that would cause them to show up on my front damn porch. Now hand me this damn bag so that I can fix my baby's food and get her in the bed." I griped as I grabbed the bag out of his hand.

Looking at me with wild eyes, he raised his hand and slapped me to the floor. As I fell down, I bumped the console table, causing a vase to drop and shatter.

"I'm over here making all these motherfucking sacrifices for you, and you are going to try to kick a nigga while he's down. Why don't you shut the fuck up sometimes??" he shouted as he stepped over me.

Hearing something drop and shatter, Taji jetted out of her room and saw me on the floor. She ran to my aid, and I assured her that I was ok.

"You know how clumsy Mommy is. I'm all right, baby girl. I just fell. Go to the table and get ready to eat," I grunted as I picked myself off the floor.

"I.... I'm so sorry, Jordan," he whispered. "I don't know what the fuck I was thinking just then. I'm sorry. I did not mean to snap like that." He explained while cupping my chin.

Yanking my head away and ignoring his complete existence, I picked the bag off the floor and continued to the kitchen.

Oh yeah, motherfucker. You are going to get yours for sure.

Outside the Lines
INDIGO

I did it again. I fucked up. I let my emotions get the best of me and this time I knew that I needed help. I put my hands on her. I actually *slapped* her to the ground. I don't know what the fuck had gotten into me but I was tweaking bad. Her telling me that those Mexican niggas were looking for me sent me over the edge. I was going to take care of it like I told her but she just wouldn't leave it alone. I never meant to hit her. I just wanted her to be quiet so that I could think. I took it too far.

Over the next couple of months Jordan avoided me like the plague. I knew that she was still in disbelief that I put my hands on her. Hell, so was I. It's like she relived that moment every time she looked into my face. She looked scared, she looked traumatized.

I had done a lot of fucked up shit to Jordan, but this

took the cake. Not only did she have to put up with my lying and cheating, but now, the hitting. I could look in her eyes and tell that it was too much for her. It felt like she'd completely checked out of the marriage. *All* the way out. Emotionally and physically.

Hitting her was definitely coloring outside of the lines in her eyes.

Since the day that I blacked out on her, I tried to be on my best behavior. I completely stopped going out. If any of my homeboys needed anything from me, I made them come to the house. The Juarez brothers never returned, and I even bought a gun for Jordan so that she could feel safe while I was away. I started taking Taji to the park and to Chucky Cheese whenever she pleased. I even planned a trip to take the entire family to Disney World in the summer.

My days now consisted of work and home. No in between. I stopped drinking liquor and started opting for lighter choices. Such as beer or wine. Even though I'd done a complete 180, Jordan still seemed unimpressed by the changes. She didn't want anything to do with me or anybody that looked like me. I was a day late and a dollar short.

She began sleeping in the guest bedroom or Taji's room. Whenever I sought her out, she made up an excuse about why she wasn't in bed. She'd say that I was snoring too loud or that her and Taji were watching a movie and she dozed off. Her fucking me was now a distant memory. It was like she couldn't stand the sight of me, and I knew it. I imagined her pussy drying up every time that I walked into the room.

I thought that maybe it was because I failed to go and get tested when she told me to. I made an appointment as soon as I could and received a negative result on everything, thinking that it would change things between us. It changed *nothing*. When I told her that I was negative, it was like she became even more disgusted. Maybe me having to get tested in the first place was a reminder of all the shit that I'd done. At this point, I couldn't win for losing. Our marriage was hanging on by a thread. I loved her and I didn't want us to end but I was losing her, second by second and it hurt.

A Fresh Start

JORDAN

Indigo putting his hands on me was the nail in the coffin. I couldn't do this shit anymore. I *wouldn't* do it. I was **done**. This marriage had run its course, and I was preparing to secure mine and my daughter's future without him. I knew what I had to do and began doing it. I signed up for summer classes and started looking for a job. I was willing and ready to start over. Getting the fuck away from him was top priority because I no longer felt safe with him, so I began to go where I did feel safe. With Tick. Our interactions became a weekly thing. I spoke with him often and slid by his house whenever I needed to be properly dicked down, which was often. While we shared time together, we strayed away from conversations regarding my relationship with Indigo. Nor did we speak of any of his dealings with other women.

We truly used the time to enjoy each other in every way possible. Sexually, emotionally, and mentally. I loved having intellectual conversations with a dope boy. He began to share the most intimate parts of himself with me. His dreams and aspirations. I asked him questions about his future and encouraged him to move on his dreams and make them a reality. He was smart. Much smarter than I'd given him credit for. Tick allowed me to pick his brain in a way that Indigo never would. He wasn't aware that Indigo put his hands on me and I had no plans on telling him. I didn't want them at odds, so I kept that little nugget to myself. I knew that Tick was just as crazy about me as Indigo was. The difference was, I felt the same about Tick.

On a random Tuesday, while Indigo was at work, I swung by Tick's place for a dick appointment and a little sexy time. After we were done, I informed him of my plans to enter nursing school. This was information that I hadn't even shared with Indigo.

"I am so proud of you, Jordan. I know that you will make a great nurse. Taking care of people is what you do best."

"I sure hope so because this is what I've been wanting to do for a long time. I'm a little nervous though. What if I get into it and hate it?"

"I doubt if that is going to happen. You've been talking about being a nurse since the first day I met you.

You're going to do great. If push comes to shove and you can't handle it, then stop and find something else that you enjoy. That nigga makes more than enough to take care of your household. Shidd, the money that you make should go to whatever you want anyway. When I decide to take that leap, my wife won't ever have to worry about paying any bills. That' ain't on her, that's on me."

"I can't lie about that, Tick. He takes care of home financially. Indigo doesn't let me pay for anything. That's the way that it is and the way it's always been."

"Yeah, probably because that nigga don't want you to------." Tick stopped talking and put his head down.

"Don't want me to what, Tick? Don't stop talking now. Is there something that I should know?"

"Not at all, love. I'm just gonna say this. Don't depend on that nigga for everything. He can be reckless when it comes to money. I've seen it first-hand. I'm not on no hating shit either. I just don't want you to be left hanging if some shit goes down. I would highly suggest you putting money back whenever you can. Actually, hold on," he raised up and disappeared to the back room. Returning, he gently placed a package in my lap.

"This should get you started."

"Tick, what the fuck is this?" I questioned as I eyeballed the large brown envelope.

"Just look in it, Jordan. Then you won't have to ask."

Peeking inside, my cheeks grew flushed. It was a few stacks of cash. More money than I'd ever held in my hands. Indigo may have made that kind of money one hundred times over, but he'd never given me access to it.

"Tick, why would you give this to me? How much is this?" I asked as my voice started to crack.

"It's $25,000. I'm giving this to you so that when you truly decide to bounce, you can, and money won't be the reason that you can't. There is no pressure. I just want to help you do whatever it is that you want to do. Whether that be pay for your schooling, down payment on a new house, shiddd, whatever you want and if you need more, all you have to do is say the word."

I reached over and embraced Tick, holding him as long and tightly as possible. Looking in each other's eyes, we shared the most passionate kiss that I'd ever experienced.

"I don't know why you would do this but thank you so much. That truly was one of my worries, but I never said anything to anyone. I didn't know how I would be able to go to school, work, and take care of my baby while starting over. This concern has plagued my mind for a while now. Thank you so much, Tick. You are truly a God send."

"Girl, that's nothing and if you really want to thank me, start putting your dreams in motion," he chimed. "Anyhow, let's go ahead and wrap this up. I've got to make a few moves today and line some things up. Besides, you've got to go and pick lil mama up from school."

"Uh huh, I do but are you sure that you don't have time for one more round? Boy, you just set something on fire inside of me. My pussy is as hot as lava right now." I teased as I reached for the head of his dick.

"Jordan, stop talking shit and don't start something that your ass can't finish. Just a few minutes ago you were yelling about the bottom of your stomach. Stop biting off more than you can chew."

"I can't help it though. I love to feel your fine ass on me and in me. You're right though. Let me get up and get my shit on and get out of here." I said as I reached for my bra and panties.

Up and dressed, I left promptly to return home and get started on dinner before going to get Taji.

In Too Deep

TICK

J ordan and I became closer than I'd ever imagined. I was falling for her in a major way. It was something about her that I couldn't resist. Maybe her smell or the way that she tasted. Whatever it was had me addicted. She was becoming everything to me and her smile was what made me know that my world was good. The next time she came over to my spot, I surprised her with an engraved novelty nursing cap and a brand-new shiny stethoscope. Floored and surprised, she noted that it was the most thoughtful gift that anyone had given her. She was overwhelmed with emotion and sobbed in my arms. I made sweet love to her to cheer her up. My feelings for her were undeniable but I knew that what we were doing was taboo. I knew that it would be the end of us both if we were found out. I didn't give a fuck though.

Jordan made me happy. I threw caution to the wind and stole every moment that I could with her. Shorty had me gone, *bad*. Shidd, we had each other gone because the closer she got to me, the further she pushed away from her husband.

Indigo began confiding in me. He'd become suspicious of Jordan. He couldn't figure out what was going on in his marriage. Jordan had become super distant and didn't seem interested in anything that involved him. She no longer stopped by the barbershop to check on him to see if he needed anything. He called her often from work, which was something that he'd always done, but she rarely answered. When he couldn't reach her at home, he called her cell phone, but it went unanswered as well.

Indigo was at the end of his rope and didn't know what to do. He *knew* he was losing his wife. He also knew that he had no one to blame but himself. He felt comfortable sharing his concerns about his failing marriage. After all, I was the cool, levelheaded friend that everyone needed. I offered great advice and was a straight shooter. I wasn't nobody's *Amen* corner, but a truth teller that would give it to you blood raw. I never judged him, well not for long anyway, and he knew that I would have his back. I received a phone call one day and I knew that it was about her. These days, it was always about *her*.

"Aye Tick, man, I need to holler at you about something. Can you meet me at the barbershop around seven?"

"Yeah man, I'll swing by there. What's up? You don't sound like yourself."

"We will talk about it when you get here. I just need some advice is all and I need somebody that will tell me the truth."

'Well, you definitely called the right one. Aight man, I'll see you in a little bit."

I hung up the phone and turned to Jordan. "That was him. He wants me to meet him at the barbershop when he gets off."

"Well, what did he say, Tick?" Jordan asked.

"Not much. That he just needed some advice."

"Well, you give it to him. I told you at the beginning of this to be yourself and act normal."

"I *am* acting normal, Jordan. You are not. He probably wants to talk about how you not fucking with him anymore."

"You're probably right but that has nothing to do with you. Indigo is the reason that I don't fuck with Indigo anymore. No one else. You had nothing to do with me falling out of love with him. His actions took care of that."

"Shorty, are you really sitting here trying to tell me that all the time that we spend together hasn't affected your relationship with him? Girl, do you realize that you are here more than you are home? You don't even go grocery shopping without stopping by here for at least a second." I voiced.

"Every moment that you are away from that home and him, you are with me. I know that it has affected you, Jordan, because it has damn sure affected me. Girl, I don't think I could stop fucking with you even if I wanted to. We are in too deep." I acknowledged.

"What are you saying, Tick?" Jordan asked while peering into my eyes.

"I'm saying that I love you, Jordan, and I think that you love me. Tell me that I'm wrong. Look into my face with those big eyes and tell me that I'm wrong?"

She looked back at me and stuttered. "I... I.... I.....Shit, Tick. What do we do?"

"We do whatever we've got to do. Do you really want to be with me?" I questioned.

"Yes, I do, but I don't see how that is possible as long as he is in the picture. Shit, we would have to leave town."

"I grew up here, Jordan. Everything that I know and love is here. I'm not running from no nigga. Anyway, don't you worry about shit. I'll handle this like I handle everything else."

Jordan leaned in to kiss me. I could tell that anxiety was taking over. Shit had gotten too real and she was unsure of what her next move should be. She didn't have to worry though. I was going to figure it out.

"I'm going to head home and lie down. I'm not feeling my best. Make sure to call me and tell me what he wanted to talk about. It's crucial that I know everything that he has going on because it will tell me how I need to be moving."

"Out of his life and into mine is how you need to be moving," I chirped as I helped her up.

I stared at her, admiring her beauty and kissed her forehead. "Don't you worry about shit. We are going be ok. I've got this."

"I sure hope that you do, Tick," she whispered as she cupped my chin in her hands, kissed me, then walked out the front door.

Sage-In the House

JORDAN

After leaving Tick's house. I needed a level head and mind to help me figure out the next phase of my life. I couldn't think of anyone better that my bestie, Sonia. We were always each other's voice of reason when shit got hectic. A come to Jesus meeting was needed because shit had gotten too real and I needed to figure out if I was being irrational in my thought process.

I tore the highway up getting to her house and I arrived in just ten short minutes.

Knock, knock knock. Sonia answered the door. "Bitch, why are you outside my house banging on my door like the damn police?"

"Because I need to talk to you and use your bathroom. Is anybody in there with you?"

"Yes, and I can't let you in right now. I don't want any trouble."

"Girl, who do you have in there that you would consider trouble? Hell, I'm just trying to steal a little of your time and use your bathroom. Not start shit with anybody."

"Sage is here. She finally called me back and I told her what you said. She wanted to come over and tell me her side of the story so that I could tell you."

"Oh, well here I am. She can tell it to me," I said as I pushed past Sonia.

"There you are. What's up, Bitch?!?! You wanted to talk to me about something. Run it!!! 'Cause what I want you to do is try and explain to me why you've been fucking my husband for the last two years. Do you think that anything that you have to say is going to change the way that I feel about you, or him, for that fact?"

"Yes but——-." Sage tried to interject, but I continued.

"The both of you are snakes and pieces of shit in my eyes. I knew that you were a whore because you've always been one. I never judged you for it because I don't know what you've been through, but this was just too damn much."

"I know that it lo------,"Sage started again.

"Shut up, Sage. I've seen you fuck plenty of bitch's

niggas, but I never thought that you would do that to *me*. I don't know why my dumb ass thought that, but I did. I must be delusional as fuck because I just knew that we were better than that. I was so wrong."

"No, you aren't. I di————." Sage tried to respond.

Cutting her off again, I yelled, "This is why you have such a hard time at life and can never get ahead. It's because you are always doing bad to people who had nothing but good intentions towards you. I only wanted to help you, and you turned around and stabbed me in the back. That's really why I want to fuck you up. Yes, fucking Indigo was a major foul on your part, but what **truly** pisses me off is that I was there for you when you had nobody."

"Jordan, you've got to listen to me. I never meant for it to go this far. He came on to me and --------," Sage pleaded.

"Shut up, bitch. Of course he came on to you. He's a nigga. They will stick their dicks in anything if you let them. Him fucking you proves that point. It's what they do but *you* didn't have to take him up on his offer. You made a choice to betray me. Nobody forced your trifling ass to fuck with him. You were supposed to be *my* friend. Friends don't do that type of shit to one another. Especially when you know that I've been nothing but good to you and to him."

"I'm sorry, Jordan. I really am. Please try to forgive me.

I was doing bad at the time, and he said that he could help me pay a few bills. I didn't want to do it, but I needed the money."

"Please stop it with the bullshit. Any way that you look at it, you are **wrong**. You could have asked *me* for help. You asked before, so just stop it. I could respect you more if you just said, *Jordan, I'm sorry. It's no excuse but I fucked up.* Instead, you sit in my face and lie. I said it to him and I'm saying it to you. Both of you are going to pay for what you did to me. In this life or the next."

"Jordan, please just listen. It was supposed to only be one time. I didn't even like him like that, but he kept coming back." Sage explained.

"Sage, just shut the fuck up because you are not helping your case. Of course he kept coming back, you dumb bitch. You're an easy lay."

"You know, I oughta fuck you up right now but out of respect for my girl's house, I'm gonna chill. You know what? Get the fuck out. I know this isn't my shit but I'm putting you out anyway. Get your whore ass up and get out!!!!"

Sage grabbed her purse and stood up. She took two steps forward. I turned to Sonia and whispered, "I'm sorry, Sonia, but I *gots* to have this bitch," before punching Sage in her mouth.

I punched and slapped her over and over. She tried to get away, but I yoked her back by her braids.

"No, bitch, No. Come here and take this ass whooping just like you were taking that dick. You didn't run from the dick when you should have so don't run now," I declared as I mashed her head into the wall and drug her down to the floor. Just as I was about to stomp on her chest, Sonia picked me up like a rag doll and pulled me off Sage.

"Leave!!!! Sage, just please go, girl. I don't know how much longer I can hold her. Get the fuck out the door, Sage!!!" Sonia screamed.

Sage scurried to grab her purse and jetted towards the front door.

"You are forgiven, bitch." I yelled as the door closed.

Sonia and I took a long look at each other before the room erupted with laughter.

Getting Too Real
JORDAN

"Now, Jordan, you didn't have to do that girl like that. She was trying her best to get away from your little ass. Bitch, you really do have those hands." Sonia chuckled.

"Girl, fuck that bitch. I didn't want to do it but the more I thought about it, the madder I got. She'll be alright. I didn't do any real damage. A few of her braids came out and she may have a black eye, busted nose and lip tomorrow, but she will be ok. If you hadn't stopped me, I'd probably still be on her ass."

Out of nowhere, a sharp pain rippled through my side. It was so painful that it brought me to my knees. "Fuuuuuck, that hurt," I grumbled as I reached at my side. "Please help me up and to the couch, Sonia. I think I may have hurt myself."

"Well you did come through the damn door like a Tasmanian devil. You probably pulled a muscle in your back or something."

Sonia helped me to the couch and sauntered to the kitchen to get a glass of water and a Tylenol, hoping that it would help ease my pain.

"You ain't never lied. I need to realize that I'm not a spring chicken anymore," I said as I reached up for the tablet and glass.

As I sipped the water, the pain intensified.

"Sonia, I think something is wrong. I don't feel right. I may need you to grab my keys and take me to the emergency room. I've never felt anything this painful in my life." I grunted.

In a haste, Sonia dug in my purse and grabbed my keys. She helped me off the couch, and we loaded up into my car. Sonia sped down the highway until we arrived at the hospital. My eyes were so heavy. I was barely conscious. Running into the emergency room, Sonia grabbed the first nurse that she saw.

"Please come and help my friend. It started with a sharp pain in her side and then it was downhill from there. I think something is really wrong with her. Can someone get her a wheelchair and get her out of the front seat, please?"

I woke up in the hospital room but could barely keep my eyes open.

"Girl, I see your eyes. You're finally awake. Don't you ever do no shit like that again. You scared the shit out of me, Jordan," Sonia admitted.

"What the hell happened and why am I in this damn hospital bed?" I asked as I looked around the room.

"To be honest with you, Jordan, I'm really not sure. I just walked in here about five minutes ago. I tried to come to the back with you, but they wouldn't let me because I wasn't family."

"They didn't tell you anything?"

"Nothing at all." Sonia said.

"You didn't call Indigo, did you? I don't want him here." I spat.

"No, I haven't called or said a word to anybody. Why don't you want your husband by your side? If I was laying in the hospital and didn't know what was wrong with me, he would be the first person that I wanted."

"Girl, I'll have to explain that to you another time. Look, I want to say thank you so much for getting me here and taking care of me. I appreciate you so much. You have literally been there for me through everything. I don't know what I would do without you. I want you to know that I'm not perfect and I've done some things that you may not approve of. Please know that I never intended to purposely hurt anybody."

"Jordan, what are you trying to tell me? Like, what are you really saying?" Sonia questioned as she looked at me sideways.

"I'm saying that there is a reason why I do everything that I do. Sometimes, it's the right thing and sometimes it isn't but either way, I'm fully aware. I'm human you know."

"Jordan, you are starting to scare me. Please just tell me what you are saying." Sonia pleaded.

"I...I want to tell you, but I'm not sure if I should." I stammered.

"You know that you can tell me anything and it won't go beyond this room. We've been solid since day one. There is no need to change up now." Sonia announced.

" I know, but————-. Wait, what time is it, Sonia?"

"A quarter til three. You've been out for a while."

"Somebody has to go pick my baby up from school. Can you please go and get her? She has to be picked up by 3:15."

"Sure, do you want me to bring her back here with me or take her to her daddy?" Sonia asked.

"You can just bring my baby back here to the waiting room. Her daddy is out of pocket. Besides, I want to see the doctor first before I see anyone else and that includes Indigo."

"Ok, I'm going to go and get Little Bit and I'll be right back, ok? Then we will finish the conversation." Sonia chimed.

"Thank you, Sonia."

As soon as Sonia left the room I drifted off to sleep again. I was awakened by the doctor tapping softly on the door.

"Good evening, Mrs. Dawson. How are you feeling?"

"I'm feeling ok. I'm just eager to know what caused this."

"Well, we've run a few tests and it appears that you are severely anemic and hypertensive. You also have a slight urinary tract infection that we are treating you for at this moment. Neither is good for you or the baby." The doctor continued to talk but I didn't hear anything past *baby*.

Cutting her off, I questioned, "Baby? Did you say *baby?* Ummm....I'm pregnant?"

"Yes, very much so. We believe that is the reason for you almost losing consciousness and could also be the reason for your urinary tract infection. Babies can affect our bodies in many different ways."

"Doctor, ummm... how far along am I?" I asked while attempting to breathe air back into my lungs.

"You are about 10 weeks pregnant. Congratulations,

Mrs. Dawson. You are in great health, and we have covered all the basis. You are as right as rain, so you are being discharged. We are going to send you home with blood pressure medicine which you are to take twice a day and are to never miss. These will not harm your baby at all. You are also to start prenatal vitamins, ferrous sulfate/iron pills, and get plenty of rest. I want you to follow up with your obstetrician and be sure to take care of yourself, Mrs. Dawson. I'll have the nurse draw up your discharge papers and you should be out of here in no time."

"Ok, thank you, Doctor." I vocalized in a weak voice as I placed my hands over my stomach.

Did You Pray For Me

JORDAN

The doctor left and grief arrived. While I knew that I was done with Indigo, I couldn't help but feel guilty about my dirty deeds. After all, it was the reason that I was in the predicament that I was in. I hadn't been intimate with Indigo in months, so I knew that it was no chance that he was the father of the baby that was currently occupying a home in my uterus.

I also knew that if Indigo were to find out about my indiscretions that there was no coming back from it. Not that I wanted anything to do with him anyway. The fact remained that having a child out of wedlock with your husband's best friend would be frowned upon by any and everyone. That was a *certainty*. I needed to come up with a solution and fast. As I sat up and began to analyze the current state of my life, there was a knock at the door.

"Come in."

"Baby, what in the fuck is going on? What are you doing up in here and why didn't you call me?"

Flashing a weak smile his way, I responded with, "Indigo, you caught me off guard. I was going to call you once I got home. I was at Sonia's house when I began to feel weak and had her bring me up here to see what was wrong. I knew that you were at work and booked so I didn't want to bother you until I knew what was going on with me."

"Well, spit it out. Are you ok? What did they say?" He asked in a concerned tone.

"They said that I was anemic and have a slight bladder infection. Oh, and that my blood pressure was high. Other than that, I'm ok. I just have to follow up with my doctor. I'm fine, Indigo. Please don't fret over me. I promise that I'm good."

"Wait, how did you know that I was in here? I didn't tell anyone."

"My homeboy's wife called him and asked if I knew that you were at the hospital. She was visiting a friend when she saw your car pull up."

"Was that all they said?"

"Yes, Jordan. Was there something else that needed to be said?" he questions with a raised eyebrow.

. . .

"No, babe. I'm just upset that they bothered you for no reason. I am perfectly fine. This little ass town gets on my nerves. People are too nosy for me."

"Don't worry about all that. I'm just glad that it wasn't something more serious. High blood pressure, huh? I have told you to stop sweating the small stuff. Sometimes, you just need to let shit go, Jordan."

Yeah nigga, I do. YOU.

"I know exactly why my blood pressure was high. I went over to Sonia's house and Sage was there. I put my foot off in her ass. That's why my shit was high. I'll be fine. I'm waiting on Sonia to come back. She went to go pick Taji up for me and she's going to bring her back to the hospital. You can go on home if you want. I'll be right behind you as soon as they get here. As you can see, I've been discharged already," I said as I slipped into my jeans and slid on my shoes.

"I know that I'm not your favorite person these days, Jordan, but I'm still your husband. I'm not going to leave you in the hospital. What kind of nigga do you think that I am?"

"It's not you leaving when I'm asking you to go. Like I said, I'll be fine."

As Indigo opened his mouth to retort, the nurse walked in with the discharge papers. I desperately tried to

DID YOU PRAY FOR ME

subtly get her attention, but she wouldn't look up from the clipboard.

"Ok, Mrs. Dawson. You are being sent home with antibiotics, medicine for your bladder infection." Right as she started to recite what was on the paper in front of her, Sonia walked in.

"Jordan, I made it just in time to get Little Miss Thang. She's outside the door and she's perfectly fine. I didn't want to leave her in the waiting room alone."

Sonia looked around and saw the nurse and Indigo standing there. "Oh, I'm sorry. I was so busy running my mouth that I didn't notice that you all were conversing."

"No, no, sis. We were just finishing up," I murmured as I grabbed the papers out of the nurse's hands. "Thank you so much, ma'am. I will definitely take my medicine as prescribed and follow up with my doctor on tomorrow. I promise. If that is all then I'm ready to go."

"Oooookay then," the nurse chirped. "You all take care of yourself and please go home and gets some rest, Mrs. Dawson. It's crucial at your---------."

Cutting her off mid-sentence, I stated, "I said I got it, damn!!!! I can read. Now if it's not too much to ask, could you please leave so that I can finish getting my shit together and get out of here?"

"Of course, ma'am. I'm sorry." She quickly exited the room.

"Damn, Jordan. You didn't have to be so mean. You bit her head off a little. If I were her, my feelings would be hurt," Sonia remarked.

"Girl, she was getting on my nerves. I told her that I got it, and she just kept on talking. I'm ready to go the fuck home and lie down and she wouldn't shut her mouth. I do feel kind of bad because I know that she was just doing her job. I did too much, didn't I?"

"Yes, you did. She didn't deserve that, Jordan."

"I know, I know. Today has been a lot and I'm just tired. Shit, I'll call back up here later and apologize." I said.

"Yes, that's a good idea, Jordan," Indigo added. "Oh, and thank you, Sonia, for taking care of my Sweets. There ain't no telling what would have happened if she would have been at that house by herself. Anyway, let's go, baby."

"Sonia, can you drive my car back to my house and I'll have Indigo take you home?"

"Sure, no problem. I'll be right behind you."

We all left the hospital and my nerves were on edge again. I had to get home and get rid of the discharge papers before Indigo laid his eyes on them. On the way home, the sad realization that I was carrying another man's baby started to set in and so did the panic.

What in the fuck am I going to do? I have got to get rid of this baby. Shit, I can't do that. I don't believe in abortions. On the other hand, I don't believe in infidelity and destroying families either but that didn't stop me from fucking Tick's brains out every chance that I got.

Interrupting my thoughts, Indigo asked, "Sweets, are you ok over there? You haven't said two words since we left the hospital?"

"I'm just tired, Indigo. I think it's the anemia. It makes you tired apparently. That's all. I want to lie down."

"Don't worry, Sweets, we will be at home in no time. I'm going to make sure that you are taken care of. I can call in tomorrow if you need me to."

"Absolutely not, I don't need you at home getting on my nerves and fretting over me. As a matter of fact, after you drop Sonia back off at home, you can go on back to work. I saw your book this morning and every slot was filled. Don't miss out on that good money because of me. I am fine, Indigo. Seriously. Plus, I've got my little helper back there and she could always call you if we need you."

"Are you sure, Baby?"

"Yes, I'm positive. Just drop us off at home and go on back to work. All that I ask is that you bring home dinner because I'm not cooking shit."

Indigo laughed. "Hell, I knew that. I'll make sure that I bring home something good, too," he assured as we pulled in the driveway. Getting out of the car, he came around to open the door for me and Taji. Walking me into the house, he kissed my forehead and headed back out the door. Sonia came in for a quick second to make sure that I was good before she left.

"Thank you again, bestie. I'll call you later on when I'm feeling a little better." I said because I knew that she wanted to know what was going on. I still wasn't sure if I was ready to tell her. I mean, telling her about Tick was one thing, but telling her about Tick *and* the baby was another.

Sonia hugged me, handed me the keys, and trekked outside. She got in the car with Indigo and they were gone.

"Taji baby, do you have any homework?"

"Yes, Mama, I do but I can do it by myself. It's easy and I don't need any help. Mama, I'm a big girl. I can watch myself for a little bit. Why don't you go upstairs and lie down, and I'll go to my room to start on my homework. I heard the nurse say that you needed to get rest, Mama. I'll come in and check on you later. Ok?"

"Ok, Sweetheart. You're such a sweet and loving kid. How did I ever get blessed with the best daughter on earth?"

"I don't know, Mama. Did you pray to God for me?"

"Actually, I did," I admitted. "I prayed for a beautiful little girl like you and God gave me just what I asked for."

"Well, I'm glad that God is answering prayers. I've been praying for a baby sister. He hasn't given her to me yet but I'm not gonna stop asking."

Babygirl's last statement almost brought me to my knees. "Ok, Taji, Mama is gonna go lie down. Go to your room and keep yourself busy. Come get me if you need anything," I mumbled as I slowly trekked upstairs to my bedroom.

Help Me Please

JORDAN

I walked into the bedroom, looked around, dropped to my bed, and sobbed. I knew that I needed to get on my knees and have a serious talk with God.

"Dear Heavenly father, it's me again and before I come to you asking for anything, let me first say thank you. Thank you for all the blessings that you have bestowed upon me. Thank you for my beautiful little Sweetpea and the grace that you show me and my family. I know that I have not walked in the light that you intended for me, and I repent for all my sins. I know that my actions are the sole reason why I am in this situation. I know that I aided in destroying my marriage but I am asking for your guidance in this matter. Lord, I don't want to get rid of my baby. It's the husband that I want gone. I have been a good wife to him, but he has not done right by me. Not for a long time, probably not ever, but only you and he know the truth. I just got tired of being mistreated and I needed some kind of release from the bondage that I felt."

"I know that you despise divorce except for one reason. Infidelity. He has shared his body with a countless number of women, and I, too, have shared my body with just one. However, I know that one sin doesn't outweigh another. We are both wrong but please help me. Help me out of this. Lord please," I pleaded.

"Show me what I should do. I know you don't make any mistakes, but please show me a sign. Give me guidance. Give me a word, even if it's from a stranger. I'm lost and I need you. In Jesus name. I pray. Amen."

Getting off my knees, I picked up the phone and called Tick but quickly disconnected the call. I was unsure if I should involve him or make the decision on my own.

Jordan call that man. He has a right to know that you are carrying his seed. I didn't know if those were my thoughts or if God put those words in my mind, but I listened and picked up the phone again. Dialing his number, I let out a huge sigh and waited for him to answer. "Please God, guide my tongue and tell me what to say."

I Got You

TICK

"Hello."

"Hey, Tick, are you busy?" Jordan asked in a nervous tone.

"Not right now. I'm about to go to the spot in a sec and then head up to the shop to holla at your nigga," I said jokingly.

"Ok. Well, I'm going to tell you before Indigo does. I kinda passed out a little today and had to be rushed to the hospital. Before you ask, yes, I'm ok," she assured.

"Hospital? What the hell happened? I know that we went hard earlier but I didn't know that I put it on you like that." I joked.

"Boy please," she giggled nervously. "It had nothing to do with what happened earlier." I could hear the wind swish past the phone as if she was pacing.

"What did it have to do with? Girl, spit it out. I want to make sure that you are ok."

"Honestly, Tick, it depends on how you look at it. I'm just going to say it. I'm anemic, got high blood pressure, a slight bladder infection, and I'm two months pregnant."

She and I both fell silent.

"Tick, are you going to say something?" Jordan muttered in a distressed tone.

"Umm, yeah yeah. I'm just at a loss for words right now."

"Well, don't be. I need you to say something and please don't say something that is going to piss me off. My blood pressure is already high."

"Jordan, baby, I really don't know what to say. Like at all. I have no words."

"Let me go ahead and answer some questions for you before you even get the chance to ask. Yes, it is yours. I haven't let Indigo touch me since before I found out that he was sleeping with Sage. Even after that we still didn't make love. One of the stipulations of him and I working it out was him getting tested and he failed to do so until a couple of weeks ago. I still haven't fucked him so there is not a snowball chance in hell that this is Indigo's baby."

"Thank you for clearing that up for me. You didn't have to though. I knew that you hadn't had sex with him. He told me that you weren't fucking with him like that.

That's why he started back fucking with Imani. Like I told you earlier, that is probably what he wanted to talk about. Does he know, Jordan?"

"About the anemia and the high blood pressure, yes. The baby, no. He wasn't in the room when the doctor came in and told me. No one was, so right now, the only people that know are you and I. Speaking of that, I need to destroy these discharge papers before he finds them."

The sounds of the rustling and ripping of papers came through the phone.

"Done," she uttered.

"Damn, man. Jordan, this is crazy and kind of unbelievable. I thought that you were on the pill."

"I was... hell I am," she said as she began to weep. "I don't know what could have happened. I'm so sorry to have put us in this situation. This is all my fault, Tick. I should have not been trying to get back at Indigo. I'm no better than him. Probably worse. At least he hasn't brought any outside children home. Not any that I'm aware of anyway," she sobbed.

"Baby, don't think like that. And no, you are not just as bad as him. You could never be. I want you to stop crying. I can't let you place all the blame on yourself like that. It is just as much my fault as it is yours. If we are keeping it real, I'm not tripping. Not even a little bit. I'm actually kind of happy about it."

"Happy? How can you be happy? I'm over here scared shitless. I don't know what I'm going to do."

"What do you mean? *We* are going to have it, that is what *we* are going to do. Ain't no way that I'm going to let you kill my baby, my firstborn. Hell nawl!!"

"I don't want to, Tick, but I don't see how either one of us will make it out alive if we are found out. He's not about to put his hands on me again!"

"Again? What the fuck do you mean, *again*? That nigga hit you?" I growled.

"Uuummm, yeah, he did. A couple of months ago he slapped me to the floor. He got frustrated because I fussed at him about those guys coming to the house. I didn't want to tell you because I didn't want you two to be at odds but yes. If he would hit me for something like that, what do you think he would do to me if he found out that I was carrying another man's baby?"

"Nothing. He's not gonna do shit. Not if I have something to do with it. Listen, I don't want you stressing yourself out about this. Get some rest and we will talk about it tomorrow. I want you to come over as soon as you drop babygirl off at school. We are going to be fine. Like I told you earlier, I'll handle it."

"Tick, I know that you are that nigga and all, but you can't handle everything. I mean, this is crazy. You are his *best friend*. I am his *wife*. This has the potential to be bad for everyone. I can't see a way out of this."

"Like I said, relax, Sweetheart. I got you and if I didn't have you before, I sure as fuck got you now. You and my seed are protected, and you can believe that like you believe in Jesus."

I hung up the phone with a new desire for life and a thirst for death.

*I can't believe that muthafucka put his hands on her! I don't give a fuck what she said or did, you should never put your hands on a woman. Especially not a woman that is pregnant with my child.. It's time for somebody to give that nigga some act right. The nigga said that we need to talk. He's damn right. We do need to talk because he will never, and I mean **never**, touch her again. It will be over my dead body that he does and that's on God.*

Where is Indigo

"Good morning, beautiful." Onyx muttered as he stretched and rubbed the small of Taji's back. "What do you have planned for today?"

"Good morning, my chocolate, fine ass husband, and to answer your question, not much. I'm going to go over to Mom's house to help her redecorate her room. Supposedly, she has a man friend that's coming to visit, and she wants to make sure that it's perfect. Whoever this old cat is, she must really like him because she's been on my ass about her decor."

"Oh yeah, did she ever say who he was?" he queried as he prepared to make a mental note of the name.

"No, she didn't say any names but it's someone from our hometown. She's super excited about him though so that makes me happy. I was worried that she would be even lonelier being here with us but apparently, Mama is making shit shake wherever she is. Whomever it is, I'm glad that he's coming here for a change. She has been going back every weekend since she moved here. She said it's to sew up loose ends and see friends, but I think that it's more to it than that." I expressed as I stretched and stroked the side of Onyx's face. "Anyway, what do you have going on today, Boo? Do you have to go into the office today or will you be hanging out at the house?"

"I've got to head up there for an hour or so to finish this report that I'm working on. It won't take me long. If you want, I'll stop by your mom's when I'm done and get the little ones." Onyx suggested.

"Yes, Babe, that's so sweet of you. It's hard to decorate with them running around and getting into everything so that would truly help Mom and me out. Oh, and while you're at it, can you and the kiddos start to take the decorations off the tree? And please be careful with my glass ornaments. I don't want y'all breaking them."

"Yes, ma'am," he chirped as he leaned over and landed a big wet kiss on my lips.

"Eeewwww, Bae, I love you and all but brush that mouth before you come putting them juicy ass lips on me."

"You don't complain when I kiss those other lips in the

morning. Don't complain about these," Onyx grinned as he rolled out the bed.

Onyx didn't think that I knew that he'd been investigating my father's disappearance. He seemed obsessed with solving the case. I didn't know if that was his F.B.I. mind working or devoted son in-law taking over. Whichever one it was, I sure wished that he would leave it alone. He pressed me often with questions and had started doing the same to my mama. She paid him dust every time that he brought up my dad's name. She either said nothing or simply changed the subject. Onyx didn't push her but he kept his ears and eyes opened. I knew that he didn't have any leads because I found his little note tablet titled, *Where is Indigo?* I really wished that he'd just give up and leave it alone. That man had been gone for over twenty something years. Let him be in peace wherever he was.

Privacy not Secrecy

JORDAN

My man was coming to see me, so I'd got to get myself right. Mind, body, and soul. I ventured off to the waxing studio this morning to get landscaped. Then to the mall to get some more smell good and a few pair of sexy panties. Taji and the kids were set to come over in a little, so I hurried home to put my new finds away and get ready to enjoy my grandbabies. After all, they were the reason that I moved to Atlanta in the first place. I never thought that my strong, independent daughter would find a man tough enough to put up with her shit, but she did. I, for one, couldn't be happier for her because now she had her own family and business to mind.

Life in Atlanta wasn't so bad after all, and I was settling in quite well. I'd found tons of activities and classes to keep me busy. I had pottery on Monday and crocheting on Tuesday. I go bowling with a team on Wednesday. Darts on Thursday and hot yoga on Friday. The weekends were for the grandbabies if I was in Atlanta or for my "male friend" when I went back to Roseville. I was a busy grandmother to say the least.

It took me awhile to become accustomed to the fast pace of Atlanta and I was embracing everyday as it came. I knew that Taji was worried when I first moved because she just knew that I would meddle in her business and life. She was so wrong. I kept to myself as much as possible. I didn't ask Taji what's going on in her house because I didn't want her asking about what's going on in mine.

For years, I kept my love life and who I was dating private. For all Taji knew, I was single. Privacy was and had always been super important to me and I wasn't going to let moving to a new city change that.

My new son in-law was so intrigued about what happened to my husband. He was constantly questioning me on the events that took place that night, but I truly had nothing more to tell. I told the same story to Onyx over and over and it never changed. It didn't change because it was the truth.

"Indigo and I were at home having a quiet dinner. Our dinner was interrupted by a knock on the door. I went to answer, and a bitch named Imani appeared in my doorway

and **boldly** told me that she was fucking my husband and had no intentions on stopping. I wanted to know more so I invited the bitch in."

"Indigo saw her standing in the foyer and became livid. He began calling her all kinds of vulgar names and asked her what in the fuck was she doing here. He denied dealing with her at first but was unsuccessful because homegirl came with receipts. She knew too much about the inner workings of our life and his business dealings for it to be a lie. She also knew too much about **me** as well."

"I got pissed and jumped on the both of them. Then I ran to the kitchen. I pulled a knife on Indigo and told him that if he didn't leave that I would cut him too short to shit. He pleaded and begged me to stay, saying that he wasn't fucking with her anymore, and he didn't know why she was there. I knew it was a lie, so I got even madder. My baby heard all the commotion and came in from the kitchen to see me and her father going at it. He told Taji to come give him a hug and I told Taji to get away. My baby became so confused that she ran to her room. Indigo wasn't leaving so I went and got my gun and told them both to get the fuck out of my house and not to **ever** darken my doorstep again. Not in a million years did I think that he would listen, but he did. He left and I never saw him again. I don't know where he is, neither do I care."

I purposely left out the fact that I was on the verge of

leaving him anyway for all his indiscretions and some of mine. Indigo just made things so much easier by running off with that tramp. Goodbye and good riddance.

To me, Indigo was a thing of the past and that was where he shall remain. Over twenty years had gone by, and I rarely think about him. When I do, it's never good thoughts.

Pulling me away from my thoughts, my phone rang and *his* face illuminated the screen. Smiling, I fixed my hair and answered the phone.

My Baby Love

STERLING

"Girl, if you could see the smile on my face, I swear just the sound of your voice makes my day a little brighter," I mutter as I drag my suitcase from my walk in closet.

"Well, hello there my love." Jordan sang.

"Hey there, Sugar, are you up and moving around yet?"

"I am, I've been up since around six this morning. I had a few appointments to attend to and a few items to pick up. I'm so ready to see you, baby. I miss you so much." Jordan voiced.

"I miss you too, Baby Love, but I'll be there first thing in the morning. Did you tell Taji that you were having company?"

"I did and you know that she is nosy as hell. She is

trying her best to figure out who it is but I won't tell her. I simply say my "male friend" and keep it at that. That's all that she needs to know for now."

"Jordan, you are going to have to tell her something at some point. The girl is heading towards her mid-thirties. I think that she's old enough to handle the fact that her mama has a man."

"Well, I don't, Sterling. I'm still not ready. It's just so much to unpack. I'd rather leave it alone."

"I know, Jordan, but the truth will come out one way or another. You might as well be the one to tell her. She should know that her mother has someone to love and care for her," I urged.

"Please don't push the issue with me, baby, I'm just not ready and I don't want to talk about this anymore, Sterling."

"Okay," I conceded. "If it makes you uncomfortable then we don't have to talk about it anymore. I'm sorry for even bringing it up. If it makes you feel any better, I've got a surprise for you tomorrow. It's not huge but it's something that you've been wanting for a long time."

"Is it dick?" she questioned then cracked up laughing.

"I said it *wasn't* huge, you know Big Daddy comes with that heat so it can't be that," I chuckled.

"Oh, you are right about that. Whatever it is, I'm sure

that I'll love it. I love all the little gifts and treats that you have for me."

"That's good to know and I can't wait to see you. I love you, girl."

"I love you, too, and please call me when you head out tomorrow so that I can watch your location. I hate the traffic here. I just want to make sure that you arrive safely," she muttered as she made kissing noises into the phone. I kissed back and disconnected the call.

The Heart Wants What it Wants

JORDAN

It was time to prepare breakfast for my grandbabies and daughter. I made my famous heart-shaped pancakes along with all the fixings. Taji, Bijou, and Jr. arrived just in time for a hot breakfast. I fixed their plates, and everyone sat down to eat.

"Mama, so tell me again about this "man friend" of yours. I know that he's from Roseville but that's about all that I know."

"Taji, that's all that you *need* to know. Why are you so concerned about my love affairs? Do I ask you anything about what goes on in your house, Mrs. Taji?" I questioned in a playful tone. "Huh, do I? The answer is no. All you need to know is that we've known each other for years and that he makes me happy. I will introduce you two when the time is right."

"Mama, I just want to know what the big deal is. Truthfully, I'm happy that you have somebody that makes you happy. I just wish I could put a face with the actions. You haven't even told me his name." Taji gabbed.

"If you must know, his name is Sterling. Now, would you babies like some more of grandma's pancakes and sausage?" I questioned as I reached for another piece of meat.

"Ok, Mama. I get it. Mind my business. I won't ask about the mister again. Just know that I will be waiting patiently to meet him."

"That's fine but that won't happen this weekend. We have nonstop plans. First, we are going to the zoo, then to the aquarium. We plan on doing a little thrifting and flea market shopping. Then dinner of course. There won't be any time for anything else, Babygirl."

"Dang, Mama, you really are going to have that man hemmed up all weekend long."

"I sure am and I've got that right. As you young folk say... he's my man, my man, my man," I chuckled.

As everyone finished their food, I trekked into the kitchen to start on the dishes.

"No, Mama. Put that dish rag down. You cooked us this fantastic breakfast. The least that I can do is wash the dishes." Taji insisted.

"Taji, I don't want you to focus on the kitchen. I'd

rather you go into the bedroom and start putting it together. You've bought things to go on the wall and so did I, but I need you to help me to arrange it so that it looks fancy. I can handle the dishes," I muttered.

Taji took the kids, and they headed back to my room. I noticed Taji's cell phone ringing, so I stopped and took it to her. It was her best friend, Jade.

"Your best friend is calling you. Do you want me to answer it?"

"Mama, just let it go to voicemail. I'll call her back later. This rod is stressing me out as you can see. I keep trying to balance the curtain rod on one shoulder and it's not working, Mama. I'm tired already. I'm just gonna wait until Onyx gets here and have him put these up. Hell, he's the tall one. He may as well get some use out of that height."

"Oh, Onyx is coming over, too? I wasn't aware that he was stopping by."

"Why, Mom? Is that a problem?"

"Of course not. I love Onyx but baby, I'm just like you. I don't like the police either."

"He's not the police, Mama. He's the F.B.I." Taji said in a matter of fact, kind of way.

"Shit, Babygirl, do you think that is better or worse?" We both looked at each other and laughed.

"I'm not going to lie, Mama. I still wake up some

mornings, roll over and look at him, and can't believe that I'm married. Not only married but married to a law enforcement agent. That still is crazy to me."

"You are right, it is crazy but crazier things have happened. The heart wants what it wants. None of us know who God will put us with. We can only hope that we like him for us as much as God does. We may not end up with who we want but sometimes who we need."

"I've never heard it put like that before, Mama. I feel it though."

How Could He?

TAJI

For the next hour or so, Mama and I worked tirelessly to get the room in order. Things were looking great, and she seemed pleased.

"Sterling is going to love this. He loves a little razzle dazzle. It's so classy and you've staged it perfectly. Thank you so much, Taji."

"You're welcome, Mama. The only thing that's missing are the curtains and as soon as my husband gets here, the room will be just about done. I just need to make some finishing touches. When he gets the kids, we can head to Bed, Bath, and Beyond and pick up some odds and ends. I want to see if I can find a vase or large trinket to go on that table right there."

Just as we were about to exit the room, the doorbell rang.

"OOh Mama, there he goes right there. My man, my man, my man." I bragged.

"Girl, shut your ass up and go get the door," Mama laughed.

Onyx walked in and the kids immediately ran and jumped into his arms.

"See Mama, this is my favorite part of the day. Seeing Onyx come home and watching the kids tackle him. They love him so much and he loves them back. He doesn't just tell them that he loves them, he shows them." I expressed with a hint of sadness.

"What's wrong, Taji?" Mama asked out of concern.

"Oh, nothing. I was just thinking about Daddy and how he would always bring me candy and bbq chips home from work."

"I see. I don't know what to say to that, baby. Your daddy loved you and you know this. Just think of all the good times we had as a family."

"I try to do that all the time but the only thing that I can really think about is him leaving us and never coming back. I mean, Mama, I've gone to therapy and everything. That still haunts me till this day. I still don't see how a man can be married with a wife and child and just up and leave. That is still crazy to me, but it happened. I'm not the first little girl to have a daddy leave and sadly, I won't be the last." Tears began to form and I tried frantically to stop them.

"Come on, Taji. Let's not do this right now. I don't want you being sad. This is a happy occasion. Almost everybody that I love with all my heart is in this room. Notice I said almost because there are others that I wish were here as well."

"Let me guess, you aren't going to tell me who those "others" are, are you?"

"Nope." Mama chuckled.

"Mama, you are something else. Seriously though. Let's head out and go get the rest of the things that we need. I also wanted to get some things for your bathroom as well. It could use a little sprucing up, too."

"Onyx, we are about to head out. Can you put those curtain rods up in Mama's room please?"

"Sure, Babe, I'll get right on it." Onyx retorted.

"Thank you... I love you and I will see you when I get back home." I advised before kissing him and the kids and heading out to the car.

"Lock up when you leave, Son-in-law," Mama commanded.

"Yes, Mama Jordan, I will. See you guys later."

Karma Perhaps

JORDAN

We made a quick run and picked up the last few little things that we needed to complete the bedroom. We returned back to the house and Taji, added her finishing touches before making her way back home to her husband.

The rest of the evening was dedicated to cleaning the house from top to bottom, grocery shopping for Sterling's favorite snacks and making reservations for our outings. The next morning, Sterling called to let me know that he was leaving the house and making his way to me.

It only took him a few short hours to arrive and I was elated when his car met my driveway. "Baby, I've been waiting on you. You are a sight for sore eyes. I hope you are hungry because I've booked brunch reservations and that is what we will do first. After that, we will hit up the zoo and the aquarium." I uttered.

"Jordan, baby, you want to do all of this in one weekend? I was hoping that we would relax on today and then run around tomorrow. You know I'm not a youngster like I used to be. I'm slowing down and all that driving tires me out."

"Awww, bae. Well, I was really looking forward to checking out the aquarium, but I've got all the time in the world to do that, I guess. Since you don't want to go out what would you like to do?" I asked.

"Nothing. Nothing is good with me. We can just spend time together and make up for the time that we have missed. I know that it's only been days but days without you feel like weeks, Jordan."

"You're so sweet. How can I say no to that face? We can sit here and do absolutely nothing if that is what you want to do. I bought all your favorite snacks so we can just relax and watch a few movies."

"Sounds good to me, Baby Love," he whispered as he snuggled my neck. "Now let's get in this house and get this Nothing Fest started." Sterling chuckled.

We spent the weekend cuddling, reminiscing, making love, and watching reruns of *B.M.F.* We loved that show because we grew up in a time when the shit was really happening. Although I wasn't privy to how the dope game really went, I was around it enough to be able to appreciate the hustle that the two brothers had. It made me think about Indigo and his crew running things. Those days were long gone.

I was now so far removed from that kind of life that it made me cringe to think about it. Also, that wouldn't be a good look especially with my daughter being married to an F.B.I agent. I knew that he had the potential to dig up every little secret that I had. I prayed often that sleeping dogs would stay sleeping and that Onyx never got a wild hair and decided to dig into my past. What he would find would for sure blow my world to pieces. Truthfully, I liked him, but I preferred to avoid him whenever possible. I didn't want him to become intrigued and start digging.

Our weekend together came to an end and he left Sunday night, headed back to Roseville. I hated that he couldn't stay longer but he had to return to work. I was retired. Sterling was not. He worked in and owned an accounting firm that demanded a lot of his time. He could never stay away from that job for long without being summoned back. I didn't mind. I loved a hard-working man. The biggest problem was the distance, but we were doing our best to make it work.

Sterling left and I decided to call my best friend to

check in on her. When Sonia's nephew raped and assaulted Taji all those years ago, we stopped talking for ages. I missed her terribly, but I was angry with her for questioning my daughter the way she did. She reached out to apologize and we worked on repairing our friendship. We were now back thick as thieves.

"Sonia girl, what's happening? I haven't heard from you in a while."

"Hey, Jordan. I was just thinking about you. I was going to call you yesterday, but it dawned on me that it was Saturday. I know that you spend Saturday with your boo, so I didn't want to bother you. I know that the time that you spend with him these days is precious." Sonia expressed.

"You're right, friend, it is but I will still talk when you call. Especially because I'm not there anymore and we rarely get time to see each other. You're going to have to bring your ass up to Atlanta to visit me sometime. I've got this big old townhouse all to myself. I would love the company. Anyway, how are you doing these days?"

"I'm ok, girl. Just working and relaxing. That's about all that I can do. I just got off the phone with my sister. She's still hooping and hollering about Marcus's ass. I know that he was her baby, but I told her that there was no need for all that crying. That boy was a monster. He was my nephew, and I loved him, but I just had to tell her the truth. The world is better off without him and that's real. I bet you didn't know that he'd raped two women in the short time that he was out and the police were actively looking for him when he broke into Taji's house. There is no telling what he would have done to Taji if she hadn't protected herself."

"I know, Sonia. I hate to even think about it. I'm glad my babygirl was prepared though. She got that shit from her daddy because before him, I hated guns. Living with a dope boy will make you glad that they exist."

"Oh, I saw your old man in town the other day. Girl, he is looking good. You know you really changed him for the better. He got his shit together quick and never looked back. I'm gonna tell you something, too. That man loves you down, baby. You are all that he talks about. He held me up in the grocery store talking about how he couldn't wait to get to Atlanta to see his baby. I just want to know the secret, Jordan. What do you be doing to these niggas?" Sonia gabbed.

"Shit, the same thing that I did to them when I was younger. Put that pussy in their face and make it talk to 'em." We both cackled. "I'm serious, Sonia, I make it talk to them. I may be in my early fifties but hell, I'm not old and I definitely don't feel old. I keep myself busy and flexible," I giggled.

"Imma see if I can put my legs behind my head and make my pussy talk. I'm going to have 911 on speed dial because this bad ass hip of mine is probably going to pop out of socket." Sonia cackled.

I screamed with laughter. "Hahahahaha... girl, you are so crazy."

"I'm so serious, Jordan. Stop laughing." She chirped while laughing herself.

"Jordan, do you remember that time that Indigo got mad at you because you wouldn't answer your cell phone and came and drug you out the club?"

"Remember? How could I ever forget some shit like that? I was so embarrassed, Sonia. Some of his homeboys tried to tell him that he was wrong, but he didn't care. He picked me up like I was a damn child. I was so mad. Then he took me home and fucked me like he hated me. That's what he always did when he knew he was wrong. Fuck the madness out of me. That shit stopped working after a while and when it did, he didn't know what to do."

"That damn, Indigo. Do you ever think of him?" Sonia questioned.

"I do but not often and when I do, it's always bad shit. Never good. Once he was out of my life, I finally felt free. It was like I was breathing for the first time. Shit, it took him leaving for me to learn who I was again. Who would have ever thought that a husband running off on his wife and kid could be such a liberating thing for me? I was able to get back to my old self. You know the smiling Jordan, the happy Jordan. I'd completely lost myself in him. Anyway, enough of his ass. Where is your better half?"

"Girl, Bane is where his ass always is. Back there watching Sports Center as usual. Not studding my ass. I'm about to get off this phone and go fuck with him and piss him off before I head off to work. I'm on second shift now and I hate it, but we are saving up to take a trip to Aruba this fall. I've gotta make this money, Jordan. Anyway, I love you and I will talk to you later."

"Love you too, Sonia. Bye, girl,"

Hanging up from Sonia, I checked Sterling's location and saw that he was just hitting the interstate. I knew that it would be at least a few more hours before he arrived at home, so I decided to take a nap in the meantime.

I was startled awake when my phone began to ring. It was my honey.

"Hey, love, you must have made it." I said as I smiled into the phone.

"Hello, Ma'am, are you Jordan Whithers, the wife of Sterling Whithers?" a voice asked.

Trembling, I answered, "Yes, I am. How may I help you?"

"Ma'am, we are calling because your husband's phone was found near the scene of an accident, and you were listed as an emergency contact. I wanted to let you know that he was taken by ambulance to Roseville Medical Center."

"Is he ok? Please tell me that he is ok. Sir, is he alive? Can I talk to him? Is he conscious? Please tell me something." I pleaded.

"I'm so sorry, ma'am. I don't have more information for you other than he was transported by ambulance. That is all that I know."

"Thank you, sir." Frantic, I hung up the phone and called Sonia's cell phone.

"Sonia, Sonia, can you hear me? Sonia, someone just called me and told me that Sterling was in a car accident and that he was being transported to the hospital. Can you please go and check for me? Please tell me that he's ok." I wept.

"Slow down, Jordan, we received an alert that we have three people coming in from an accident, but they haven't arrived yet. We are preparing the rooms now. I will call you back as soon as I know something." Sonia promised.

"Don't worry, I'm on my way," I muttered as I hung up the phone and called Taji.

"Listen, I don't have any more information than what I'm about to tell you so please don't ask. Sterling has been in a car accident close to home, so I am leaving right now to go be with him. Ok, baby?" Not waiting for a response,

I hung up. Running to my room, I quickly packed a duffle bag, threw my keys and cell phone in my purse, and headed out the door.

Putting the petal to the metal, I turned a four-hour trip to Roseville into a three-hour trip. I ran into the emergency room and requested to see my *husband*.

"Ma'am, I am Mrs. Whithers, Sterling Whithers' wife. I was told by an officer or a paramedic that my husband was being brought to this hospital. Could you please look on your books and let me know what's going on?"

"Oh yes, I'm aware of the accident. Just give me a few minutes and I'll get right back with you. Why don't you have a seat in the waiting room, and I'll try to get more information for you," the nurse stated as she grabbed my hand and walked me to the waiting room entrance.

The nurse left briefly but returned and told me that Sterling was in surgery. She advised that he was very badly injured and would probably need several surgeries to correct the damage that was done. Sterling suffered a fractured skull, a broken pelvic bone, hip, and femur bone, and shattered his ankle bone. He also had several deep lacerations, a collapse lung, a busted spleen, and a compressed spine. He was in very bad condition. Upon hearing the news, I couldn't breathe, and I fell to the floor.

"This is all my fault. If he would've never come to Atlanta, this wouldn't have happened. I should've never asked him to come. Oh my God, what have I done?" I screamed.

The nurse did her best to comfort me, but I was inconsolable. "Oh God, help me please!!!" I cried.

"Ma'am, ma'am, please come with me. I will show you to the ICU waiting room. It is usually empty in there and that way you will have some privacy," the nurse offered.

"No ma'am. I don't want to go to the waiting room. Show me where the chapel is, please." I commanded.

The nurse patiently walked me down to the chapel and left me be. I prayed and begged God not to take my husband. I prayed for so long that I eventually fell asleep on the chapel altar.

The chaplain awakened me.

"Ma'am, would you like to come and pray with me?" he asked.

"Yes, pastor, please. Please pray that my husband doesn't die." I requested with a face full of tears.

"I'm sorry, ma'am, but that's not how it works. What I will do is pray that God's will, be done. If it is in His will for him to live, then your husband will live. This is all that I am able to do." The chaplain bluntly explained.

"Now sir, you are lucky that we are in this chapel because if we weren't, I would lay you out right now. Where is your compassion? Your kindness? What kind of man of God would say that to somebody? I am a Christian as well and I would never tell somebody that I won't pray for them." I scoffed in disgust.

"I never said that I would not pray for your husband. What I said was that I would not pray for him to live." he repeated.

"You know what, I heard what the———."

The Sweetest Symphony

TAJI

"Mama," I screamed from the doorway. Cutting her off mid-sentence. "Don't you say that to that man. Mama, come here." I commanded.

Thankfully, she walked away from the chaplain, cutting her eyes at him as she ran towards me.

"Hey, baby, I'm so glad that you came. I came down here to pray but this mutha-----."

"Mama, don't say it. I know he upset you, but we are in a Chapel. Don't worry about him. I will pray with you. Do you mind if Onyx comes in as well?"

"No, of course not. We need all of the prayers that we can get. Sterling is in very bad shape. He broke so many bones, baby, I don't know if he will ever be the same. It's all my fault Taji," Mama stated.

"No, it's not, Mama. There was a witness downstairs that saw the accident. Sterling was less than a mile away from town. He was run off the road by another vehicle and hit another car head on. It was a freak accident. The driver of the vehicle that ran him off the road was experiencing a medical emergency. They wouldn't tell me what kind of emergency, but he didn't make it. Mama, I know that this is hard to hear, but Sterling *did* make it. He's alive. Let's just be thankful for that." I urged as I embraced my mother, hugging her tight. Onyx wrapped his arms around the both of us, and we stood there in the chapel weeping and moaning.

While embracing one another, I heard crying coming from outside the chapel. A young lady bust through the door and fell to her knees. Mama looked up and ran over to her. She embraced the young woman and got her to calm down. Onyx and I looked on from afar when I heard...

"Mama, why didn't you call me? Why didn't you call me to tell me? Is my daddy gonna be OK?"

Startled at what I'm hearing, I walked over and interrupted the young lady.

"Now wait a muthafucking minute." I said while sucking my teeth. "Did she just call you *Mama*?" I questioned.

"Taji," Onyx yelled. "You are in a chapel. Don't use

language like that. Didn't you just fuss at your mama for doing the same thing?"

"Onyx, please, not right now, baby. I need for this young lady to explain to me why she's calling her Mama." I narrowed my eyes as I walked closer to the young lady and my mother.

Mama looked up with weeping eyes and muttered, "She's calling me her mother because I *am*....her Mama. Taji, this is your sister, Symphony."

"Sister, Mama? What are you talking about? Sister? Are you kidding me right now?" I gasped.

"No. Not at all. We are technically in the church, and I wouldn't lie to you in a church. This is your sister and Sterling is her father."

I could not believe what I was hearing or even what I was seeing. I took off, running out the chapel doors until I found the nearest restroom. I stepped into the first stall and sat down on the toilet, breathless, confused, and angry.

She's always talking about telling the truth and integrity and she has a whole baby that she's hid for years. That girl has got to be in her mid-twenties. What the hell is going on? I'm gonna go back out here and she's gonna give me some answers now.

"Taji, baby, please come out. Please. I can't come in there because that's a woman's restroom. I need you to come out here and talk to me. Tell me what you are feeling." Onyx yelled through the door.

"I can't right now, Onyx. I just can't."

I faintly heard my mama's voice through the door. "Yes, you come on in here, Mama. You and I have to talk because what in the hell do you mean your daughter?" I yelled through the door.

Walking in, Mama asked me to come out of the stall.

"Listen, baby girl, I know that you have——-,"

"Are you sure you want to call me *Baby girl* because she sure as hell looks younger than me?"

"I know that you are angry, but there is so much more to it than you know, Taji, and I promise that I will tell you the truth and nothing but the truth when the swelling goes down. I cannot do this right now. You certainly deserve an explanation, but please don't make me do this. I don't possess the mental fortitude." Mama maintained.

"Mama, do you really expect for me to go back to the house and get a good night sleep knowing that my mother has kept a whole baby away from me? Like how? When?"

"I promise you that I am going to answer all your questions. Just give me a few moments to collect my thoughts. There is so much going on right now. I swear to you, baby, I will tell you the truth, all of it. Just not now!"

"OK Mama, I guess I don't have much of a choice. I

can't force you to tell me anything but just know that I will be waiting with bated breath for an explanation."

"And you will get it but first, I need to go check and see if there has been any progress with Sterling. Let me go ahead and tell you this now because I don't want this to be another slap in your face, but my last name is not Dawson any longer. It's Whithers. Sterling and I are married. Your father was presumed dead seven years after he went missing and was unheard from again. We got married on the 8th year. We have been married for 16 years."

My mouth dropped to the floor.

"I know, baby, I know. It is a lot to take in and process, but once I tell you the full story, I do believe that you will understand. You are grown now, and Sterling has been urging me to tell you for years, but I was afraid. I guess now there is nothing to be afraid of any longer so you will know everything."

"Oh my goodness, Mama. Is this a damn Lifetime movie or something? I cannot believe this, but OK, I'm going to wait. While you sit here and wait for information on *your* husband, Onyx and I are gonna go back to the house. Please call my cell phone when you have time."

"Oh, one more thing," Mama gritted. "Ummm, your sister now lives in the house, but of course you can go there anytime you want. I told her that she may use any room besides the master bedroom. You and Onyx are welcome to go there."

"Mama!?!?!? You mean to tell me that you gave her the house, too?"

"No, baby, I didn't give her anything. Your father and I bought that house. She asked me could she move there while she was furthering her degree in accounting and business management, and I agreed. I'm sure that when she's done, she will buy a house of her own. Then we can rent it out. That house will go to you in the event that's something happens to me. It belongs to you and me only."

I shook my head in disbelief.

"Taji, please don't hate me. Please, baby. I'm sorry for not being honest with you. Are you mad at me? Would it be too much to ask for a hug?"

"Mama, I could never hate you. You've been too good to me but if I'm being honest with you, yes. I'm mad as hell so no hug for you. I still love you. You are still my first lady, but I am the maddest that I have been in a long time. As soon as we get somewhere stable, I will be calling my therapist and setting up a session immediately. Don't worry about us staying at the house. Onyx and I will get a hotel room."

"I know, Sweetheart. I understand you not wanting to stay at the house. Trust me, I deserve everything that you're going to give me."

"Yes, you do."

"While you are setting up therapy sessions, you can set me up one, too."

"One more question, Mama. Shall I include Symphony in our sessions? I'm pretty sure she's going to need them."

We both stared at each other before I cut the tension with a slight smile.

"OK, Mom, Onyx and I are going to take off and we will talk to you later."

Go Home Mama

JORDAN

Sterling's first surgery was a success despite the injuries that he sustained. I spoke with the doctors at every chance and refused to leave his bedside. He was placed in a medically induced coma. The medical professionals explained that it was better this way as it would allow his brain and body to heal without interruptions.

My heart literally hurt every time that I glanced over at the tubes and the cast that covered most of his body.

"Sterling, I know that you can hear me, baby. I want you to know that I need you. *We* need you. Symphony is a mess. She doesn't know if she's coming or going but she misses you terribly. That's why you've got to fight and come back to us. Oh, and you'd be happy to know that Taji finally knows everything. Well, almost everything. I really hadn't had the time to give her the exacts but she does know that she has a sister and that you're my husband."

"I would be lying if I said that it wasn't the shitshow that you'd always said it would be, but she took it better than I thought that she would. I'm going to sit the both of them down at some point and explain everything to them. In the meantime, I want you to get better, baby. We've got so much shit to do. What about that trip to Thailand that we've always talked about? Or getting that Bungalow in Bora Bora. Or simply watching our grandchildren grow up."

I began to sob at that thought. Symphony had yet to have any children and the thought that their grandfather may not be around to see them into this world broke me. My grandchildren already had a grandfather missing from their life. I hated to think of it happening a second time. While sitting at his bedside and holding his hand, Taji and Onyx trekked into the room.

"Mama, I know you want to be here for him, but you've got to go home at some time and bathe. This room is rank, and I doubt if it's him."

"Taji, now how dare you say something like that to me? I'm your mama. How are you going to walk in here and not even say hello? No hey or nothing. Just Mama, you stink."

"I promise you that I'm not trying to hurt your feelings, but Sterling isn't going anywhere. All of the nurses and the doctors that you've spoken with told you that he was stable. He's good for now. We will stay here with him. Just please go home, bathe and put on some fresh clothes. And don't forget to comb your hair while you're at it. I've never seen you look a mess like this."

"Well, tell me how you really feel, Taji. I guess my outsides match my insides. I am a mess, my dear. You would be, too, if Lord forbids, Onyx was laying up here with tubes everywhere and a cast covering his body. They have him wrapped up like a Mummy. The places that aren't covered by a cast are covered with bandages and gauzes. I absolutely hate to see him in this condition. I can't even see his face to give him a kiss."

"Would you really want to, Mama? You haven't brushed your teeth since this happened. I thought that you wanted him to live. Not kill him," Taji grinned as she slapped her knee.

"I'm glad that you can find some humor in this because I sure can't. Girl, I am sad and hurt down to the bone. This is my man, my best friend. I don't know what I would do without him, and I don't ever want to find out." I expressed.

"We know, Mama, but seriously, we've got him. Just go

home and get yourself together and come right back. I'll call you if you are needed in any way, ok?"

"Ok, Baby. I'll leave since you are telling me that I smell like a pole cat. Now I'm wondering if the nurses and doctors have noticed. Anyway, bye," I said as I hugged Taji and Onyx and exited the room.

Conflict Resolution

TAJI

Onyx and I sat and conversed amongst ourselves. I still could not believe everything that had happened and could not wait for Mr. Sterling to awake because I had a few questions for him as well. Like, did he know my father? Did he ever want to meet me? So many thoughts ran through my mind, and I was dying to let them out.

"Speaking of your father, I wanted you to know that I met with the chief of the Roseville Police Department regarding his case but came up empty-handed. There were no witnesses, no evidence, no paper trails. Nothing. It was as if he disappeared into thin air."

"Why are you just now telling me this, Onyx? I told you that I didn't need for you to investigate anything regarding my father. He made his decision and left. That was all that I needed to know. As far as I'm concerned, I don't have a father. I was laid by a buzzard and hatched by the sun. Now I really wish you would leave this alone."

"Looks like I am going to have to because this is one of the coldest cases that I've ever seen. Anyhow, did you call Symphony back?" Onyx asked. "She's been calling you for three days straight. I don't understand why you won't return her phone call."

"Because Onyx, I just don't want to right now." I groaned.

"It is not her fault, **none of this** is her fault so don't treat her like an outsider when she isn't. She is your *blood* sister, and I really don't like this side of you, Taji. I know you are stubborn as an ox and hardheaded but taking it out on your little sister isn't going to do anyone any good. You always complain about having a small family and here is your chance to expand it. I know that it was shocking to discover that you have a sister, but I thought that by now, you would have tried to embrace it and get to know her a little better."

"Onyx, please don't lecture me right now."

"Well, somebody has got to. You are wrong and I'm going to tell you that you are wrong. I am your husband and not one of your little friends. Have you ever sat and thought about how *she* feels? Knowing that she was virtually *a secret* all of her life."

"She wasn't a secret to everybody. Just to me. Her and Mom seem to have a good relationship and the way she was in here hollering about Sterling, he couldn't have been too bad of a father. This is why I'm pissed off because I feel like everyone lied to me. Everybody knew about her except me. Even Miss Sonia. I saw her downstairs at the nurse's station. She spoke and dropped her head."

"I seriously doubt if that had anything to do with what's going on now. I mean, Taji, you did kill her nephew. Maybe that's why she put her head down because she didn't want to look you in the face. There could be a myriad of reasons why she didn't say anything. This is a difficult time for everyone right now, so don't just assume that the lady is avoiding you because of that reason."

"Onyx, why does it seem like everything that I am doing these days pisses you off?"

"Because it is. Look, I come from a big family, we all have our differences, but we love each other at the end of the day. There is nothing that I won't do for any of my sisters, and you know this, so I don't get why you are acting the way that you are. Baby, you need to do some deep soul-searching and get over yourself. Everything isn't about you."

"I know that it seems as if I am not taking this very well and that is because I'm not. I don't dislike Symphony, I just don't know her, and I am still processing it all. Give me some grace, Onyx, you are my husband. My therapist told me one time that everyone doesn't deal with grief, trauma, or just everyday issues the same. This is my process, so I just wish everyone would respect it. Plus, Mama has yet to tell me what really happened and how all of this came about."

"Maybe once I get that information it would be a little bit easier to digest. I don't like when you are upset with me, Onyx, and you know I don't like to fight. So, I will give it a valiant effort, and I promise to call her when we get back to the hotel. Maybe I will invite her out for dinner and have a conversation."

"Yes, see, baby, that's what I like to hear. Conflict resolution."

"Shut up, Onyx," I chuckled. "Is that something that you learn in one of your little seminars with the FBI?"

"Actually, no, Taji. That is something that I learned by just simply living, baby."

I Told You So

SONIA

I'd been waiting to see Jordan all day. I needed to know what's happening family wise. My girl had a serious task ahead of her and I just wanted her to know that I supported her in every way. While on her way to Sterling's room, Jordan stopped by the nurse's station to speak with me.

"Hey, girl, I'm glad to see that you got your ass out of here and took some time to get yourself together."

"Sonia, I oughta kick your ass! Why didn't you tell me that I stunk? My daughter walked in the room and told me that I needed to go home and bathe. You've seen me every day that I've been here, and you didn't say a word."

"What did you expect for me to say, Jordan? Was it something like I know that your husband needs you, but you smell like day old cabbage?"

"Yes, that's exactly what your ass should have said." We both chuckled.

"Anyway, your husband is doing great according to the doctors. His wounds are healing nicely, and all of his vitals are stable. He has a long road ahead of him, but he's tough. Tick is gonna be just fine."

"No, Sonia, now you know he stopped going by Tick a long time ago. Please try to remember to call him Sterling." Jordan requested.

"Oh girl, I'm so sorry. I forgot. Well, Sterling is going to be just fine."

"I sure hope so, Sonia. Life definitely wouldn't be the same without him. Anyway, let me get my butt on up here. I know that Taji is probably ready to go."

"Ummmm,about that. She and her husband walked past here a while ago. I could barely look her in her eyes. There is so much that I want to say to her, but I just don't know how to start. I still feel bad that Marcus did what he did to her, back then and recently. I've always blame myself for it. He is the one that taught me that you never put anything past anyone. Not even family."

"Awww, Sonia. I would suggest that you have a talk with her. She doesn't bite. Wait, well she is quite feral sometimes," Jordan jokingly said. "I think that if you just sat down and talk with her that you both could come to a common ground. I've got to do the same. I still haven't mustered up the strength to tell her exactly what happened, but that day is coming very soon. My baby does not possess an ounce of patience, and I'm surprised that she's waited this long."

"Well, Jordan, you have no one to blame but yourself because Sterling and I told you years ago that you should've told her. Personally, I don't think that you should have ever sent her to your parents while you were pregnant. That would have taught her early in life that sometimes things happen that we don't expect to happen, but there is always a silver lining."

"I hate to say it, but you guys were right. She was livid at me, and I deserve it, but I'm gonna pull this family together. Anyway, girl, I love you and come see me before you get off."

"I'll be up there. Be strong, sis. God has got you."

Wake Up Love

JORDAN

I trekked to Sterling's hospital room to find Onyx and Taji asleep in the recliner.

"You two lovebirds can wake up now. I'm back and feeling better than ever. Smelling better than ever, too."

"Thank God," Taji remarked as she stretched her arms out and hugged me. "Mama, Onyx and I are going to take off. We're gonna head over to your house and see if Symphony is there. She's been calling me for a couple of days, but I wasn't ready to talk but now I am."

"That's so good to hear. Your sister knows very little about you. Yes, I know that's my fault, but you have the opportunity to present the best version of yourself to your little sister. I think you will find that you have a mini me. You both are so much alike in so many ways... more ways than I care to explain. She's a little sweeter than you, but hey, your mama still loves you."

"Mama, don't be funny. I'm not mean. Right, baby?" She turned to ask Onyx and he looked around the room.

"That's not fair. I mean, I know that I can be a little rough around the edges, but I wouldn't call myself mean." Taji pouted.

"Whatever you say, Baby. Anyhow, Symphony took off from school for a little while so she should be at the house. Go on by and make sure you call me later and tell me how it goes. I plan on leaving here tonight because my back is killing me from this chair. Sterling is stable and is going to be fine, so I plan on sleeping in my own bed tonight."

"OK Mom, we will see you later," she said as she walked out the door.

Waltzing back to his bedside, I bent down and whispered, "I'm back, baby. I told you that I wouldn't be gone for long. How about I put on some of your favorite music?"

I grabbed my phone and tiny Bluetooth speaker and put on, *That's The Way I Feel About Cha* by Bobby Womack. He loved that song and would sing it to me often.

Grabbing his hand, I danced by his bedside while I sung softly in his ear. Tears began to flow as I mouthed the words to the song. As I was dancing, I felt Sterling squeeze my hand. I stopped to see if I was really feeling what I thought I felt and realized that was just a reflex. This made me sadder than I was before and I became inconsolable. I desperately wanted to hear, *Hey, Baby Love*. I wanted to feel his hand on the small of my back. I wanted him to cuddle with me and to feel his loving embrace. Anything that he had to offer right now, I was willing to take.

As I was giving Sterling a small concert, the doctor walked in.

"Hello, Mrs. Whithers. I see you and our patient are having a little groove session," he grinned.

"Yes, Dr. Primo. My honey loves music. Especially blues and old school music. I realize that he is in a coma and probably can't hear me, but that doesn't stop me from talking to him."

"Well, you won't have to worry about that for much longer. A few of the other doctors and I have discussed it, and we've decided to wean him off the medicine to see if he will wake up. Only then will we be able to gauge the extent of the damage. Brain injuries are very difficult to diagnose and even more difficult to know whether or not he's going to return to himself. It is usually a matter of waiting, so if I could give you any advice in this matter, it would be to have patience. You're definitely going to need it. We will start scaling back on the medicine this evening and by day three, we should know a little more about the extent of his brain injury. If and when he does wake up, he may be extremely groggy. He may not know where he is or how he got here. It is very common in patients that have suffered a brain injury to experience some version of amnesia. With that being said, please don't take it personal if he doesn't remember you. He may say some things that are out of his character, and I don't want you to take those things personal either. I see that you are a very devoted wife. I just want you to know that we are doing our very best to help your husband so if you need anything from us, just let us know."

I hugged Dr. Primo and thanked him once again for all of his help. Within a few minutes, a nurse came in and administered medicine to his I.V. She turned to me and said, "It's a waiting game from here. Be patient," and left back out of the room.

I played song after song for Sterling in hopes that one of his favorite songs would encourage him to wake up and jigged to it.

From the Horses Mouth

F our hours had passed before I decided to leave Sterling for the night. It was at the end of Sonia's shift, so I asked her to accompany me to the house while I talked to the girls. I knew that I didn't have the strength to do it alone, and since Sterling was incapacitated, Sonia was the next best thing. She'd been there with me through it all. Sonia agreed and followed behind me as I made my way to the family home.

Once I arrived, I noticed that there was only one car in the yard and that was Symphony's vehicle. *Dammit, Taji has already left. I guess I'll have to try this again tomorrow.*

Sonia and I entered the house to find that no one was there. I called Symphony's cell phone, and she told me that she was at dinner with Taji, but they were getting ready to leave. I informed them that I was home and waiting for them to come so that we could finally have this long-awaited conversation.

Taking the phone from Symphony, Taji told me that they were on their way back and hung up.

Within minutes, I heard the motor cut off in the front yard, and my stomach began to churn. The moment that I'd been dreading for years was finally here and I had nowhere to run. It was time for me to put my big girl panties on and faced what I'd done.

The three of them came piling in and took a seat on the couch. All eyes were on me. Sonia took a seat in the recliner, pulled out her phone, and started scrolling on the Internet. She was in an awkward place as well but wanted to be there for me.

"OK. Before I begin, let me get some things out of the way. I am wrong. I have been wrong for a long time, but I want you both to know that I take accountability for however you end up feeling after the truth is out. I have done some things in the past that I am not proud of, but if I had to be honest, I don't regret one single thing."

"Taji, I'm going to start with you. You are the oldest and I know you must be confused about a lot of things. I want you to leave here with a clear mind and heart if possible. You are going to hear some things about your father that may surprise you and anger you. But rest assured that everything that's going to come out of my mouth is 100%

my truth. I will not lie to you. All I ask is that you all wait until I finish before you start with the questions. In other words, please don't interrupt me. I will allow you to ask me whatever it is that you want once I'm done, but you must let me get it out."

"Do we all agree?"

Symphony and Taji both nodded their heads.

"I want you to hold on for the ride because this is going to be a long one."

"Taji, the first thing that you need to know is that I loved your daddy fiercely. When we first got together, he was like a knight in shining armor. You know how the story goes, a woman meets a man, he sweeps her off her feet, they fall in love, get married, and start a family. That is essentially what happened. Baby girl, I'm not sure how much you remember about our life back then, but your daddy was a kingpin. That's how we were living good and how we bought this house. When we were dating, I asked him about the rumors surrounding him being one and I told him straight up that I couldn't be with someone who was hurting our community. He admitted to me that he was and that he was getting out of the game. And I believed him. But, of course, that was a total lie. He actually got deeper into it. I don't believe that he ever intended to leave the game. Especially when those Mexican niggas dropped by the house one night, scaring the hell out of me. Anyway, lemme stay on track. Shortly after we got married, I found out that your father was cheating on me. I forgave him and tried to work through our marriage and move on with our lives. That proved not to be a smart decision of mine because he continued to cheat. Over and over and over again. Not only was he a compulsive cheater but he was also a compulsive liar as well. Excuse me for saying this, but Indigo was a *fuck nigga who did fuck nigga things*. Even then, I loved him."

"Well, eventually I got tired of it and decided that I was going to get a little get back."

Taji side-eyed me with a smirk.

"Don't look at me like that. I am human like everyone else, and I fucked up. Anyway, against my better judgment, I decided to pay your father back for all of the hurt and anguish that he caused me. What better way to do that than to sleep with *his* best friend."

Taji and Onyx's mouths dropped open. Symphony put her head down and looked as if she wanted to disappear into the couch. I noticed but I continued.

"It was only supposed to be a one-time thing. Just a way for me to get back at Indigo for doing the things that he did to me. Initially, after I slept with the homie and got my lick back, I was *done*, and we attempted - for the umpteen time - to work on our relationship, our marriage.

I tried, I mean I really did try to trust him again, but it was hard."

"Indigo swore that he wanted his family and was willing to do whatever he could to keep us. For a minute, and I do mean *a minute*, your father seemed like he was changing his ways for the better. He stopped drinking, he stopped going out to clubs, so I assumed that he was on the straight and narrow. He wasn't."

"At that particular time, he was still sleeping with two women, and Sonia can attest to everything that I'm saying. Once I found out that he was still cheating on me, I went back to his homeboy and continued to sleep with him. We started to spend just about every other day together. We began getting to know each other on a deeper level and eventually, we fell in love."

"He was kind, he treated me well, and he wanted the best for me. I was **done** with your father and his bullshit. So, I decided that I was going to start nursing school and leave Indigo. I mean, he wasn't going to ever stop cheating on me. He wasn't going to ever be the man that I needed him to be. Baby, he had become downright horrible and was sucking the life out of me. I was becoming just a bitter shell of myself."

"The last straw came when he slapped me to the floor. I checked out immediately because I don't play that hitting shit. He had done so much damage to our relationship and our marriage that I felt like there was no coming back from it. I signed up for nursing school and prepared myself for a future without him. The homie gave me $25,000 to put away so that when I decided to leave, that it would be easier. Your dad was the sole breadwinner at the time and I didn't have the same access to the change that he did."

"Things were falling apart just to fall into place. Just the way that I needed them to. That was until I found out that I was pregnant."

And Then...

JORDAN

"Your father and I hadn't slept together in over 3 1/2 months. Why you ask? Because I found out that he was fucking a nasty slut named Sage, who I once considered my other best friend by the way, and another slut named Imani, and I refused to open my legs to him. I asked him to go get tested and he did not, so I kept my pussy to myself."

Everyone in the room had a bewildered look on their face.

"Y'all don't have to look at me like that. We are all grown. Anyway, I knew that it couldn't be his child, so I toyed back-and-forth with what I was going to do. Sterling told me that I was going to have his baby because there was no way in hell that he was going to let me get rid of his seed."

I looked over at Symphony, making sure that I had her complete attention before making my next statement. "An abortion was **never** on the table, but he told me off rip that that wasn't even an option. Sterling and I started devising a plan on how we were going to tell Indigo but in the meantime, I had to act normal until we had everything figured out."

"About a week after I found out that I was with child, we were all sitting down having dinner. Taji, I'm sure you remember this. We were eating, when there was a knock on the door. I hopped up to answer it and one of the sluts that he was fucking had come to my home, boldly told me that she was sleeping with my husband, and that she had *no* intentions of stopping. I pulled a knife on him and asked him to leave. He refused and said that she was lying. Imani was not lying because she came with proof. Receipts after muthafuckin' receipts. After he wouldn't leave, I pulled my gun on him and told him and her to get the fuck out of my house and not to ever return."

"This is how I know that our words have power because after I said that, I never saw your father again. Never. I have no idea where Indigo went or where he's at. Imani disappeared as well so we all assumed that they ran off together. This may hurt to hear but I didn't give a damn where he was. As long as he wasn't here. By that point, all the love was gone. The last smidgen of love that I had for him left the minute that he slapped me to the floor. I felt at the time that he did me a favor by leaving."

"I filed a missing person's report and attempted to move on with my life, but it was hard. When summertime came around, I started to show. Symphony was growing and I started to panic because I didn't know how to tell you that I was pregnant with another man's baby. Taji, even though you were young, you were super intelligent. Now I know that this was stupid, but I didn't know what else to do, so I devised a plan to send you off to stay with my parents until Symphony was born."

"Once she was born, I came and got you from my parents and Symphony lived with Sterling in the house that he purchased for us. . He, by no means, was a single parent. I spent as much time with Symphony as possible while you were at school. I would go over in the mornings and be with her until you came home. While I was there with her, I would often pump breastmilk so that Sterling could feed her when I was away. On the days when Sterling was busy or she got sick, I brought her with me and told you that I was babysitting for a friend."

"No one knew that Sterling and I were together as a couple, and we co-parented very well. We did not go public with our relationship, simply because he was Indigo's best friend and everyone in town would have looked at me like a slut. I didn't want to be shunned. Indigo was dark as night and Symphony not only looked exactly like Sterling, but she was also light bright like him and I.... I know this is a cowardly thing to say, but I wouldn't have been able to handle the backlash."

"We did everything in our power to stay a secret. This was against Sterling's will. He wanted to scream it to the world, but I resisted. It was my decision and my decision only to keep your sister from you. Sterling wanted you two girls together from the very beginning, but I didn't want you to hate me, Taji. I know at that age, if you would've found out that I was cheating on your father, you wouldn't have been able to understand the whys. I just knew that you would hate me and blame me for your father leaving when that wasn't the case. He left on his own accord. He just happened to leave at a time that benefited me the most because I didn't have to explain to him what I done. He left and never knew that I was pregnant with Sterling's baby."

Taji looked me in the face and blinked wildly.

"Hold tight, baby, I'm almost done. When you went off to college, I moved in with Sterling and I'd been living with him ever since. I had my calls forwarded from the house to the house that I shared with Sterling. That's how I was able to answer every time you called me. When he pissed me off or I just needed some alone time, I would simply go back to my house. Everything worked out perfectly. When you called from school and told me that you were coming home for the weekend, I would simply trot on back to the house. Sterling hated it, but I guess I'm like you in a lot of ways. Stubborn as a damn mule."

"Now you all can stop looking at me like I have four heads and go ahead and ask your questions because I know that they're coming," I chirped as I grabbed my cup of water and took a sip.

Mama Smashed the Homie

TAJI

"You know, Mama, I am completely flabbergasted but you laid it out pretty well for me. Everything was easy to understand except for one thing. You kept saying that Sterling was dad's best friend. I was old enough to remember dad's best friend and his name was Uncle Tick. Not Sterling. Where is Tick? Whatever happened to him?"

Sonia looked over at me and let out a deep sigh.

"Ummmm, Taji, *Sterling is Tick*. He no longer goes by that name, but yes, baby. They are one in the same."

"Mama!!!! Uncle Tick? How could you? Like seriously, how could you do that? Listen, I am not the one to judge anything because Mama, you don't know half of the things that I've done. I'm not gonna sit up here and act like a prude but damn!!!! You mean to tell me that

Symphony's father is *Uncle Tick*. Now I see why you didn't want me to know because you're right, there is no way in the hell at nine years old that I would have been able to understand that. I am at a loss for words and that never happens."

"It sure as hell doesn't," Onyx chimed.

"Hush, Onyx. Anyway, you are telling me that Uncle Tick is laying in that hospital bed?"

"Yes, Taji. He is your "Uncle Tick." I said in a matter-of-fact way.

"You cheated on my daddy, had a baby with, and married his best friend. Wow, just wow. I don't even know what to say, Mama. I don't think I have any questions right now. I'm going to need about a week to sit on this egg."

"I told you it was a lot. You don't have to talk to me right now and I can understand if you don't want to talk to me for a while. Now you know the truth and the whole truth. I have literally told you everything step-by-step. This is truly how things went. Since you don't have anything to say just yet, let me turn to my other sweet baby because I've got things that I need to say to her as well."

A Tattered Soul

JORDAN

"Symphony, baby. I know that sitting there, listening to it all had to be a lot for you as well because you didn't know any of that either. I'm sorry that you had to find out this way but first, let me make one thing clear. You may not have been planned, but you were *not* a mistake. I loved you from the moment that I found out that I was carrying you. I loved my little baby bump and loved you even more the moment that I held you in my arms."

"Your father and I lied to you a lot. I know that all of the times that I wasn't there, you thought that I was working as a traveling nurse. I did work, that wasn't a lie, but I was essentially living a double life. I took care of you during the day and Taji at night. I tried to give you the best life I could, even though I wasn't in the same house with you."

"Trust me, it really hurt me not to be. I pray that you understand why I did the things I did. I had two children that I loved more than anything on this earth and two very complicated situations that I had to deal with. I tried to be there for you both as much as I could. You know that your father would scorch this earth about you and if you didn't know, I would as well."

"I kept you away from your big sister and that was wrong of me, so wrong, but I'm hoping that you two can build a relationship and love each other just as much as I love you both."

"Mama, I've never doubted your love for me. Although you were "working," I never felt like I missed out on anything. You were there when I needed you and that's that. I do have questions though. So, Mama, please forgive me for saying this, but Daddy was your side nigga?" Symphony questioned.

We all burst out laughing.

"If you wanna put it like that, yes, he was my side nigga, but not for long. He stepped up and became *the main* and we never look back. Sterling has been one of the best things that ever happened to me."

"Mama, I've got to give it to you. You were able to keep this up for a long, long time. I hate to say it, and please don't take this as disrespect, but you had to be *a bad bitch* to pull something like that off." Symphony uttered.

"Symphony, I was thinking the same thing, but I wasn't going to say it," Taji laughed.

"Was and is. Like I said, I am not proud of a lot of the things that I've done but I don't have any regrets. I have two beautiful, successful girls that I did my damnest to raise with love. I don't think I did a bad job. I have to admit, my soul is a little tattered. All the lying and sneaking around got the best of me at times. Trust and believe, I get on my knees every night to pray for forgiveness for all the wrong that I've done. It feels so good to get that off my chest and to see you two together."

"It sure the fuck does, Jordan," Sonia blurted out. "I've been wanting you to do this for so long and I'm so glad that this happened. I'm not glad at what happened to Sterling but out of a bad situation came some good."

"Yes, it did, Sonia." Jordan concurred.

Clearing her throat, Sonia spoke. "While we are confessing our truth, let me get in on this. Taji, I want to say to you that *I am sorry*. Sorry for so many reasons, but I will start with my nephew. I never thought that Marcus was capable of doing such things and I should've believed you the first time you said it. You know I was raised to always protect family and that's what I was trying to do. Nothing more. I know that me questioning you when you told your mother that you were raped, hurt you in the process. For that, I apologize."

"Your mama put those paws on me though and got me right." Sonia chuckled. "To be honest with you, I knew that you weren't lying when you said it, but I just couldn't admit it. Admitting it would've meant that it was ultimately my fault because I brought him around you. I introduced him to the family. I should have known better, but hindsight is 20/20. When I see you and put my head down, it is not because I am upset with you. It is because I'm *ashamed*. I know that you did what you had to do, and I don't hold any ill will towards you for protecting yourself. If anyone broke in my house and stalked me, I would have done just what you did and wouldn't have thought twice about it. I love you and I have always loved you since the very first time your mama showed me your beautiful little face. I just needed you to know that before this night ended."

"Thank you for saying that, Miss Sonia. I love you, too, and there are no hard feelings here either. You've been my Auntie Sonia since I could remember. I could never hate you. I tell my best friend, Jade, all the time that she should not apologize for anyone else's actions and although you are my elder, I'm going to tell you the same thing. You had *nothing* to do with Marcus being a complete fucking psycho. At the end of the day, he did what he felt he had to do and so did I. What's done is done and I'm not mad at anybody. Not anymore anyways."

"Good, baby. I'm glad to hear that you are healed from that situation. Now let me turn my attention to my sweet Symphony. I've been in your life since you pretty much came in this world. I've always wanted the best for you. I never wanted to see you hurt in any kind of way, which is why I urged your mother every chance that I got to tell you the truth. I don't want you to sit here and think that I wasn't advocating for you because I was. I am your Godmother after all, but your mama is just hardheaded as fuck."

"I get it, Miss Sonya. Yes, you are my Godmother, but you were her best friend first and foremost and you were just doing what you were asked. No one blames you for anything and just like Taji, I still love you. That will never change. After all, you gave me my first Chanel bag," Symphony giggled.

"Wait a minute, Auntie Sonia," Taji gasped. "You out here giving out Chanel bags? Where in the hell is mine?" Taji queried while giggling.

"Ummm... Mrs. Ma'am, I know you aren't asking me for a Chanel bag. Your mama told me about your mansion and your fancy cars. I know you got money to get your own, hell, you could probably buy all of *us* one." Sonia chuckled.

"Well pop my balloon, Auntie Sonia. I was just kidding anyway." Taji chirped.

"MAMA," Symphony uttered. "This has been a long day. I've got a lot of thinking and processing to do. I am going to take a bath, get into this bed, and try to get some rest. I plan on going and sitting with Dad first thing in the morning. I can't wait for him to wake up. I've got so many questions for him."

"Me too!!" Taji exclaimed. "So many questions because how are you gonna bust down my daddy's old lady like that?"

Symphony snickered.

Taji turned to Onyx, "Now I see where I get all of the fuckery from. Here I was thinking my mama was a *saint*. I called myself moving her from Roseville so that she wouldn't be lonely and she's got a whole damn daughter and a husband over here. Once again, I played myself."

"Baby, don't look at it that way. You were looking out for your mom's best interest. As fucked up as it may seem, I truly feel like she kept all of this away from you because she thought that she was looking out for yours. The only thing to do now is accept and move on."

"Mom, Symphony was right. It has been a long day. My head is spinning. Onyx and I are going to head out.

First, we are going to stop by the liquor store because I think I need a bottle of Casamigos, then we are going to go back to the hotel. I'm going to have me a shot or six and go to bed. We have one more day here before we go back to Atlanta. Jade has my babies, and I miss them so much. I'm ready to get back to them."

"I know you are, I'm thankful that you came to see about your mother and make sure that I was OK. You and Onyx didn't have to come, but you did, and I appreciate you being here for me. I love you, Baby girl, and you two drive safely back to that hotel."

"OK, Mama, we will do and I love you, too. See you tomorrow," she said as she exited the front door.

We Did It Joe

JORDAN

I stared Sonia in the eyes and shook my head.

"You finally did it, bitch. That was a long time coming, and I have to say, it went way better than I thought it would." Sonia voiced.

"Me too, Sonia. I was so damn scared. I thought those girls were going to jump up and whoop my ass... together as a family," I cackled.

"Seriously, Jordan, I expected for them to be upset, but they had to realize that you were in a tough spot. A spot that you put yourself in but a tough spot none the less. I still remember the very day that you told me you were pregnant with Sterling's baby. After you left that day, I went back into my house and just stood in the kitchen for 10 minutes straight, staring at the wall and praying. I was in complete shock."

"If *you* were in shock, imagine how I felt?" I chimed.

"Jordan, I never told you this, but I just *knew* that Indigo was going to kill you both. I would often have nightmares about him doing something to you. He was a mean motherfucka at times."

"Yes, he was and I'm glad his mean ass is long gone. Him and that Bitch."

"Girl, there were so many rumors going around about what happened to Indigo because of the way everything went down. I mean, he left his businesses, the properties, and everything that seemed to mean the world to him."

"Some people said that you had him killed, some people said that he fled the country because the Juarez brothers were looking for him. Some say that they killed him. Every other day, it was another story about what happened to Indigo. That shit was the talk of the town for years." Sonia recalled.

"Yeah, it was, and I was so glad when motherfuckas stopped talking because I was tired of hearing it. Police officers were stopping by my damn house, FBI agents, and old girlfriends. His mama and daddy never believed me. They just knew I had something to do with it but I didn't. It was just all too much. I would have crumbled if it wasn't for you and Sterling. You are talking about pressure, that was **big pressure**."

"Well, sis, you made it through and just like those girls,

I'm about to get the hell on out of here and take my ass home. I am tired and I have to be back at the hospital first thing in the morning."

"OK, Sonia, thank you for being here with me while I did this. I needed the support."

"You know that I'm gonna always be there for you. I'll holler at you later. Take care," she said as she left.

I locked up the house and glided into the master bedroom. Just about everything that I owned from this house was either sold or back in Atlanta. The only thing that I left behind was my old bedroom furniture. Standing in the middle of the floor, memories of Indigo and I dancing invaded my mind. I quickly pushed them out, laid down and drifted into a deep slumber.

Symphony woke up before I did and headed to the hospital to be with her father. She left a note on my bed, letting me know that she planned on spending the complete morning with him. Citing that I should get rest, sleep in, and then come to the hospital around noon.

Waking up, I read the letter and took Symphony's advice and slept in. That was until I heard a knock at the door. Grabbing my housecoat, I answered.

"Hi, how may I help you?"

"Hello, Mrs. Whithers. My name is Moné Marie and I help run the accounting firm with your husband. We got news of the accident the next morning and we've wanted to reach out, but we weren't sure if it was appropriate. Do you mind if I come in and talk to you for a moment?"

"Oh sure, pardon my manners. Please come in," I said as I took a step back and allowed her to stroll in. "Moné Marie, was it? Please have a seat."

"Thank you so much. I'm not going to take up much of your time. I'm sure that you are busy, but I just wanted to ask if you don't mind if I took over the day-to-day operations of the business. Sterling has a huge workload and at the moment, it is piling up. Do I have your permission to take over some of his accounts?"

"Do you not care to know how your boss is doing? You're here asking about taking over the accounts, but not one time did you ask about my husband's wellbeing."

"Ummm, I... I," Moné Marie stuttered.

"Are you aware that his daughter does the exact same thing that he does? He was the one to teach her so if anybody will be taking over the accounts, it will be her. There is not a paper that you could get me to sign to turn over all of the hard work that my husband has done to someone that I've never heard of," I stated as I shifted my body towards Moné Marie.

"I'm so sorry, Mrs. Whithers. I wasn't trying to upset you and I can understand how it seemed insensitive, but we've all been kind of on edge since this happened. Most of his clients only want to deal with him and it has been a struggle to even get them to consider one of us."

"I wonder why that is. Is it because you all can't be trusted or because you lack tact and personability?" I said wide-eyed.

"What is that supposed to mean, Mrs. Whithers?"

"Just what I said, baby. I don't beat around the bush or mince words. Can you all be trusted?"

"Of course we can. I've been with the firm for eight years and Christian has been there six years. Listen, I think we got off on the wrong foot. We adore your husband, and we only want the best for him and his business. We are just trying to keep things moving forward. We heard that the accident was pretty bad and that Mr. Whithers would be out of reach for a while. We are just trying to keep our jobs and keep the business afloat."

"And if that is what you are trying to do, I truly appreciate it, but don't worry, I'll have Symphony come down there immediately to sort out her daddy's business. Now if you don't mind, I have to get dressed and get to the hospital to see my husband." Standing up, I waited for Moné to get the hint and do the same.

She eventually did and I motioned towards the door. Moné Marie promptly left.

Moné in the Middle

JORDAN

S hrugging my shoulders, I bathed, got dressed, fixed a cup of coffee and an English muffin, and headed out the door. Once I arrived at the hospital, Symphony and I spoke about what occurred back at the house.

"Symphony, have you heard of a Moné Marie? I'm asking because she came by the house right before I got ready to leave, talking about taking over your daddy's accounts."

"Oh noooo, none of that will be happening. Don't you worry about it, Mama. Once I leave here, I will make my way to office to get started on his accounts. I never did like her. Every time I would go visit Daddy, she looked me up and down like she had an issue with me or something. She almost got slapped across the face a few times, but Dad did what he always did. Diffuse the situation."

"Is that so? I find this strange because I've never heard of her, but she said she's been there for years."

"She's not lying, Mama. She has but I still don't trust her, and I have a feeling that Daddy didn't either. I get along better with Christian."

"Well, you get your butt down there as soon as possible and thank you so much Baby girl for looking out. Call me later and tell me how it goes." I said as Symphony was on her way out the door.

"Sterling, your Baby Love is back. I had a good night sleep, and I couldn't wait to get back up here to be next to you. Oh, and we have to talk about this little Miss Moné Marie."

"Do you know that that little heifer had the nerve to come by the house, not *our* house but *my* house, and ask me could she take over your accounts? In so many words, I told her **hell no** because baby, I don't know you. Please don't worry though. I sent Symphony down there to take care of everything."

"She's got you and me in her, so you know she's going to get some straightening. I don't want you to worry about anything but getting better, Sweetheart. You hear me in there? Get better, my love. The world is such a better place with you out there fucking up in it," I giggled to myself.

"The biggest news of all though comes from last night. I had a long-time coming conversation with Symphony and Taji. I must say, Sterling, you would've been proud of me. I was nervous, but I kept my cool and told them the truth and nothing but the truth. They were a little in shock, but that was to be expected."

"I thought that they were gonna gang up and whoop my ass, but they didn't. Sonia was there for me as usual because you know she's my road dog and got my back. Now that they know everything, baby, you've got to get better. There is so much left for us to do and so much love that we have to give."

"Oh, and don't think that I forgot," I muttered as I pulled out my Bluetooth speaker.

I put on Pandora and told it to play music by Johnny Taylor. The first song that came on was *Running Out of Lies.*

Running out of Lies

STERLING

I vaguely hear *Running Out of Lies* by Johnnie Taylor playing. It sounds like it's miles away, yet I could hear it clear as day. It's a strange feeling but above the song, I heard my Baby Love's voice. What I couldn't understand was why I couldn't see her? I also didn't understand why moving my arms was a huge task for me. They felt like fifty pound weights. My fingers were twitching and so were my eyelids. After a minute or so of trying, I managed to get them open and my Baby Love was standing beside my bed singing her heart out. My toes began to twitch as well but she was so engulfed in the song that she didn't notice.

"Indigo, that's Indigo's song," I said but my voice was barely a whisper. The music began to sound distorted, and

I believe that I fell out of consciousness. *What in the hell is going on with me?*

I now felt Jordan at my bedside. She lowered herself down to my level and called my name. I answered, but she didn't notice. It dawned on me that I was talking, but my mouth wasn't moving, neither were my limbs or any other part of my body. My eyes were open, but for some reason, I couldn't see her anymore. I didn't know if I was in or out of consciousness. This revelation caused me to panic and my eyes to buck with fear.

"Jordan... Jordan... Baby Love, help me. Can you hear me? Baby, please say that you can hear me."

"Well, ain't that 'bout a bitch? Help you? Nigga, ain't nobody coming to help you. Just like nobody came to help me." A familiar voice muttered.

"Look at her, she's beautiful, she's free, and right now, she might as well be single. What the fuck could you possibly do for her in the position that you're in? Shiddd, you'd be better off dead like me. At least she would grieve over your ass. My head wasn't even cold before she moved on and had a baby with you. You were supposed to be my main nigga. My ace boon coon."

"Indigo, is that you? Man, what the fuck is going on? Am I dead?"

"I don't know, motherfucka. Are you? You know, out of all the low down, dirty son of a bitches in town, I would have

*never thought in a million years that **you** would be the one fucking my wife. If somebody had told me that it was you, I wouldn't have believed them. I probably would've knocked their asses out, scalped them, and called their mama a ball headed ass lie."*

"Indigo, it wasn't like that man. I promise you it wasn't. Jordan came at me. And the only reason she came at me was because you were dogging her out every chance you got. Nigga, I told you that she would get tired of that shit and she did. That's not my fault." I expressed.

*"Tick, man, I'm not trying to hear that shit. Even if she did come at you, **you** were supposed to be my boy. You could've had any bitch in the street. Why did you have to pick **my bitch**? My Sweets, you know how I felt about her."*

"Indigo, I was your boy, true enough, but you and I both know that she was always too good for your ass, man. Look at you, even now, you are calling her out of her name. You never loved her. You never treated her right. So, I decided to step up and be the nigga that would."

*"Yeah, but you left out one detail. You had to **murk** me first. I bet you she doesn't know that, does she? You got her thinking that you're some kind of fucking savior. You ain't no better than me.. You were just better at hiding it."*

"Indigo, I'm nothing like you. I'm more man than you could have ever been."

"Well, I guess we will never know now, will we? You took

that from me. How about this... If you are such a good man, then why don't you tell her what reallllly happened to me. You got her thinking that I ran off with some bitch and that I left my baby behind. I mean, yeah, I was doing what I was doing with these other hoes, but I would've never left my baby. In fact, I would've never left Jordan. You will tell her what happened to me."

"Right now, I can't tell her shit. I can't even talk."

"Yeah but that's only temporary. You will be able to talk and when you do, you better tell her, Nigga. If you don't, you will never have another peaceful night on this earth, and I'm going to make sure of it!!"

"Indigo, Indigo, what does that mean?" I continued to call out Indigo's name but there was no answer. No sound, no light, no nothing. Just pure darkness until it wasn't. Seemingly in the flash of an eye, I woke up. I still could not move from side to side, but I was able to open my eyes. I opened my mouth once again and called Jordan's name. This time, she heard me and she leaped from the recliner and to my bedside.

"Sterling, you've been in and out for days now. I am so happy that you are awake. It is so good to hear your voice. It's a whisper but a voice none the less. Welcome back," she said as she leaned down and kissed me.

My face felt numb. As bad as I wanted to feel her lips on me, I could not. I was able to move my toes and fingers but still nothing else. I saw that I was covered in cast on different parts of my body. Which would explain why I couldn't move anything. I wondered if the cast wasn't there, would I be able to move?

"Baby Love, what happened to me? How did I end up like this?" I queried.

"You were in a car accident, Sterling. It happened about a mile away from downtown. A driver experiencing a medical emergency hit you head on. It was bad and I'm not gonna sit here and lie to you, baby. You've got a long road ahead of you. I just want you to know that I'm gonna be right here by your side."

"Why can't I move? Am I paralyzed?"

"Not that I'm aware of, but you may be weaker on one side of your body. You have some spine damage. Sterling, you have so many injuries that it hurts me to even talk about them. You can't move because you are essentially in a whole-body cast. Moving could make your injuries worse. I'm going to let the nurses and the doctors advise you of your injuries and how they plan on treating them."

I looked up at her beautiful face and I couldn't help but cry. Tears pooled in the corners of my eyes.

"Noooo, nooo, don't cry. You are **alive** and that is what matters. You have breath in your lungs and your heart is still beating which means you still have a chance."

"How long ago did this happen? How long have I been in here?" I asked in a voice no louder than a whisper.

"Not long, Sweetheart, a little over a week. They had you in a medically induced coma, but they wanted to see how you would react if they took you off everything. You have a skull fracture, but from the looks of things, you seem to be yourself."

"Can you please get a nurse in here?" I requested.

"Yes, I can, and I will in just a minute. I just have one question before I leave out this room. Could you hear me talking to you?"

"Yes, I could. I heard you tell me how much you loved me. I heard you tell me that you told the girls the truth, I heard you playing all that good music, and I also heard Taji tell you that you stunk. Believe it or not, I was laughing, but of course no one could see it."

"Damn, Sterling, you didn't have to bring up that part. Anyway, I'll be right back. Oooh, I'm so happy," she shrieked as she ran out the room.

Tell Her

"I hear you talking, Nigga , but you ain't saying the right shit. You better tell her." Indigo's voice vibrated in my left ear. "You are in here, smiling and shit, all in love with **my** motherfucking wife, knowing that you put me in the dirt. TELL HER!!!"

"I am, nigga, damn. Give me time. I just woke the fuck up. I'm trying to figure out what the hell happened to me."

"Fuck what happened to you. Tell her what happened to me!!!"

"Leave me the fuck alone. I'm going to get to it," I scoffed, attempting to raise my voice.

"Who were you just talking to?" Jordan asked as she entered back into the room.

"Myself. I just can't believe that all of this happened. I'm thirsty as hell and my mouth is dry as a bone. Do you think that they will give me something to drink?"

"I don't see why not. I can go get you some ice chips, but the nurse said she'll be down here in just a few. How are you feeling? Are you in any pain?"

"Jordan, I feel like I've been hit by a car, *literally*. Pain isn't a good enough word to explain how I feel. This is pure misery. The only solace that I have is seeing your face."

"I'm so sorry, Sterling. I hate to see you laying here like this."

*"But I don't. Nigga, you are **exactly** where you're supposed to be. In fact, you're supposed to be next to me."*

I ignored the voice and tried to focus on Jordan. I had a limited range of motion so unless she was close to my bed, I could not see her.

"Come here, baby. Come over here and sit on the bed next to me please. Can you hold my hand for me?" I asked.

"Of course, I'll do anything that makes you feel better."

Jordan sat down on the bed and grabbed my hand. She leaned over directly in front of my face. As I looked up at her, I saw Indigo standing behind her.

Jumping out of my skin, my eyes widen as I blinked

heavily, trying to make sure that I saw what I thought I saw.

"What's wrong, Sterling? Is there something hurting you?"

"Nawl, baby, that motherfucka saw a ghost. Ain't that right, Nigga?"

"Shut up!" I shouted.

"Sterling? Who in the fuck are you telling to shut up? All I did was ask you was there something hurting you."

"I'm sorry, Jordan. I wasn't telling you to shut up. I was talking to myself again."

"Well, baby, you aren't in your head anymore. When you talk to me, I can hear you. If you want somebody to talk to, I'm right here. Just say what you need to say."

*"That's right, motherfucker. Say what you need to say. Tell her what you did to me. Tell her how you set me up. Tell her **everything**."*

Ignoring the voice, I confirmed, "I know you are, Jordan. I'm sorry. I am just overwhelmed right now. How long is it going to take for the nurse to get here? Can you please go back up there and tell her that I need to speak with her now? I need something to calm me down. I'm feeling a little uneasy. Also, I would love to see my girls. Symphony *and* Taji. Can you call them and tell them that I'm awake and please ask them to come up here?"

"OK, whatever you ask. I'll be right back."

*"Ohhhhh, you done trained my bitch real good, huh? Got her around here calling your bitch ass Sterling and shit. Your name is Tick, and it will always be **Tick**. It's the perfect name, too. It fits you so well. A blood sucking motherfucka that doesn't know when to quit. Did you know that a tick will continue to suck even after it is filled to the brim? They die, still sucking blood, long after they are full. Sounds just like your ass."*

"Indigo, please just stop; I haven't trained her to do anything. We have a mutual respect for each other. Something that you knew *nothing* about." I quipped.

*"Oh yeah? Let's see what kind of **respect** she has for your ass when she finds out what you really did. Since you are all perfect and shit. Mutual respect for her, huh? Does she know about the shit that you were getting into while she was in Atlanta with my grandbabies? Grandbabies that I will never get a chance to hold or talk to or take fishing or do anything with, you low down dirty son of a bitch?"*

"Indigo——!!! God dammit."

"Don't call my name like you're going to do something. What the fuck can you do? You about three steps away from where I am. You can't do shit. All I want is for you to tell her the truth. Like I told you, you won't get a peaceful night on this earth if you don't. TELL HER!!!!"

Jordan sauntered back into the room. "They are a little

tied up right now, baby, but they'll be here shortly. Most of the call lights were going off up there. You must have forgotten. I am a nurse, too. If there's anything you want to know, just ask. Oh, and I sent a text message to both girls, and they will be up here shortly. Symphony went over to Taji's hotel room to see her off, but I caught her just in time."

"Good, I finally get to see those two together. I hate that I'm in the condition that I'm in, but I know that will bring me joy."

"I'm sure it will, baby. Symphony is ready to see her daddy and Taji is ready to give you a full interview," she chuckled.

"I'm ready to answer any questions she may have. Taji is a lot like you. She is hell on wheels, and I know she's gonna give me the business. Full body cast or not."

"I'm glad you know. I hope you don't take any offense to whatever may come out my baby's mouth, but after me lying to her for so many years, I get it."

"Yes, and I'm going to tell her that it was *you* lying to her all these years. Not me. I told you to tell her 1000 times." I softly chuckled.

"She knows, Sonia told her already. She wants to know how on earth could you be her daddy's best friend and be fucking on his wife?" Jordan laughed.

"She said that?"

"Yep. And you know she's gonna ask you, too. She is like me, she doesn't mince words."

"Dammit, that nurse needs to hurry up and come here with some water and anxiety medicine because she's gonna have my blood pressure up."

Close Your Eyes
STERLING

"Sterling, do you want my advice?"

"Yes, baby, I do," I retorted.

"Just be honest with her. Tell her the truth. It sure as hell set me free when I was able to speak mine."

"I will. After all, I have nowhere to go and I sure as hell can't run from her, so I've got to face her."

"That's right, Nigga. You do. Your day of reckoning is here," Indigo boasted.

There was a soft knock at the door and a nurse walked in. "Well, good to see you awake and alert, Mr. Whithers. How are you feeling?"

"I sure as hell have had better days, I am in extreme pain. I'm also extremely anxious, I don't know whether it is because I cannot move my body, but I am feeling really antsy. Is there something that you could give me to take the edge off?"

"Sure it is. Let me go speak to your doctor and see if we can draw up an order right fast. Did your wife advise you on your injuries?"

"She did not. She wanted you all to tell me so let it rip. What's all wrong with me?"

"Oh my, Mr. Whithers. Where do I begin? Well, first, you have a fractured skull, a busted spleen, a broken pelvic bone, hip bone, and femur bone. Your ankle was shattered as well. You have several deep lacerations, a collapse lung, and a compressed spine."

"Damn, all that. That's why I'm breathing all funny, huh? That sounds like a lifetime of healing and arthritis." I chuckled.

"Could be, Mr. Whithers. Only time will tell. You may be here with us for a while and then eventually, you transfer out to a rehabilitation center. I hope you don't have any plans."

I laughed, "Well, I did, but I guess those don't matter now. Anyway, back to this pain medicine and anxiety medicine. Can you please go see about that?"

"Sure, give me a little time and I'll get you right."

As the nurse left out Symphony and Taji walked in.

"Where is my son-in-law?" Jordan asked.

"He's downstairs in the cafeteria, feeding his face. He said he felt like this was between us so he's going to chill out down there until we are done over here."

Symphony ran right to me.

"Daddy, I am so glad that you are awake. I prayed so hard this morning while I was here with you. I prayed that you would wake up with all of your memory intact because boy do I have some questions for you."

Everyone in the room laughed, including me.

"I know, baby, your mama told me that she told y'all everything last night. Now, listen, I will answer as much as I can, but when this nurse comes back with this medicine, I'm probably gonna be out again. I am in so much pain. Y'all don't even understand."

"Well, Mr. Sterling/Uncle Tick. You don't have to worry about me running a list of questions down for you. I only have one."

"Go for it, Taji."

"Now, why on earth would you pick *my mama* out of all of the women in the world to mess with? Don't get me wrong, I was a little girl when you were around, but my memory is superb. You were at the house all the time with Daddy. I remember that every time he made a move, you were right there beside him. What would convince you to start messing with his old lady?"

I grunted and cleared my throat. "There is a very simple answer to that question. I want you to look over at your mother and tell me what you see."

"OK, I can do that. I see a beautiful woman, strong and resilient. She never lets anything get her down and if she does get down, she doesn't stay there. She's full of life, full of love. I see confidence, I see happiness all over her, especially now that you're awake. I see my mama in her best light."

"Now I want you to think back to when you were a little girl. I want you to close your eyes and envision your mother. What do you see then?"

Taji closed her eyes. She didn't say anything but let out a deep sigh. She began to weep. Then she spoke.

"I see me and her watching movies all the time, alone. I see frustration on her face and sadness. I see her trying so hard to be happy, but nothing ever seemed to work. I see the look on her face every time my dad left the house. I see fear. I see resentment. I see sadness. I see unhappiness."

"Open your eyes, Taji," I commanded.

"All the things that you saw when your eyes were closed were all of the reasons why I did what I did. The woman that your mother is now is a reflection of the tenderness and love that I showered her with. Not your father. I don't want to talk badly about him, but he wasn't right for her. He took her for granted and took advantage of her kindness every chance that he got. I fell in love with her and all I wanted to do from that moment was protect her and make her smile. I have literally spent the last 25 years of my life doing just that. Baby, I know it was wrong, but the heart wants what it wants and in your mama's case, her heart needed what it needed. I'd like to think that that was *me*. I am not saying what I did was right at all because I'm sure if your father were here, he definitely would not agree."

"You damn right I don't agree. Fuck all that shit you talking. Throwing salt on my name to my baby girl. Nigga, if I could reach out and touch you right now, I would. Instead of a few bones being broken, I'd break your ass in two."

"So Taji, I hope and pray that you can forgive me for my transgressions. I never meant to hurt your family. I only wanted to love y'all and better yours, my babygirl's, and your mother's lives."

"Uncle Tick, as messed up as it was for you to have done what you did, I completely understand it now. No one wants to sit around and watch someone that they care about be mistreated. Thank you for caring for my mother the way that you have. In turn, I know that she'll take great care of you. I really, really hate to run, but I've got to get back to my babies. Hopefully, you'll get a chance to meet them. I love you, Mama. Symphony, I'll call you tonight, and Uncle Tick/Mr. Sterling, I truly do hope that you get well soon. We've got a lot of catching up to do as a family." Taji walked over and hugged Symphony. They embraced for a while, and Jordan joined in.

Then, Taji left out the door.

"My sweetest Symphony. Is there anything you wanna ask your daddy?"

"Nope, you've answered it all. I still can't believe that you were a side nigga though, Daddy."

"Me either," I chuckled.

"Daddy, is there anything that you need for me to do?"

"Yes, tell me what's going on at that office."

"Oh, I went down there this morning, and they had already moved some of your accounts to their computers. I moved them right back and told them not to touch another thing until I had a chance to go over it. I left for a little bit to go be with Taji. As soon as I leave here, I'm going to go back up there and if I have to stay all night, I'm gonna get everything in order. I know that you're going to be out of commission for a while, Daddy, but I don't want you to worry. I am going to get things back on track. I'm still in school, of course, but I take a lot of my classes online so I will still have time for both. Also, my professors know about the accident so they understand."

"Symphony, if things get too hard for you or if it becomes too much, you let me know. I have a couple of good friends that I trust to go in there and take over in my absence. You don't have to do it all by yourself. Christian is definitely the next go to in that office if you need some help."

"Christian is the only person that I see when I go into the office because I walk right past that chick. I know that if I say two words to her, we gonna be thumping in there so I try to keep my distance."

"You *are* your mother's daughter, that's for sure. Always trying to fight somebody."

"I'm just saying, Daddy. I don't like the way she looks me up and down. Like if you wanna do something, just do it. Now that you aren't there, there's nobody to pull me off her ass."

"Symphony, there is no need for all of that. Please don't turn my office into a MMA match. As a matter of fact, Jordan, do you know where my phone is?"

"Yep, baby. It is in a Ziploc bag in the drawer next to you."

"Can you please charge it, turn it on, and find Sonny Thibodeau's number and call him for me? I'm gonna have him come up there and help you get those accounts in order. He owes me a huge favor."

"Oh, I remember Mr. Thibodeau. I like him, he's so funny." Symphony voiced.

"Yes, he is a character, but this is about business. Those

accounts are important, and I need them to be handled as such."

The nurse walked back into the room and clicked on her little computer for a few minutes. She let me have a few sips of water before giving me two shots into my I.V. Within minutes, I was out again.

I Got This

Symphony and I left the room and retreated to the waiting room so that he could rest. We sat down and discussed all the things that were going on right now.

"Symphony, you and I haven't had any one-on-one time since all of this has happened. Baby, how are you emotionally? I'm asking because I worry about you. You are so young but yet, you take on so many responsibilities. Are you sure you're up to doing this accountant thing at your daddy's firm? You know you can say no."

"Mama, I got this. This is a small thing to a giant. Plus, my daddy needs me. What I look like letting him down in his position. He has never let you or me down."

"You're right about that, Sweetheart, but I just wanted

to make sure that you knew what you were getting yourself into."

"Of course I know, Mama, and you also know I love a challenge. I've got this, I promise. If I see that I don't have it, I will let you know. Have they come out with a medical plan for Daddy yet?"

"Baby, he just woke up. We haven't even seen the doctor yet. He should be making his rounds pretty soon and we will figure it all out, but don't you worry. There ain't nothing going down without me knowing about it first. I worked at this hospital for years. They are going to treat him like royalty and if they don't, they will have my foot in their asses and they know it."

"Mama, your little bitty self is always threatening somebody."

"Baby, those don't be threats, those be promises. You better ask your Auntie Sonia. Your mama got hands for real." We both cackled.

"Mom, I really like Taji. She is the coolest big sister ever. She told me that she had over seven bedrooms in her new house and that I could come and visit whenever I wanted."

"And you can. She used to always beg me for a baby sister. Now she's got one and I know that you all are going to be tight."

"I hope so because she just seems so real, like me. A no nonsense type of chick and you know I love that."

"She is baby, but she dealt with a lot of traumas in her past. I'm not gonna go into detail. I will allow her to do so if she feels comfortable but just know that Taji you see now is a result of years of therapy and that beautiful husband of hers."

"I didn't wanna say nothing, Mama, but that man is beautiful. I'm talking about fine, fine. He looks like he was carved. That's how perfect he is."

"Symphony, you can't be looking at your sister's man now. That's a recipe for disaster. You are your daddy's child," I teased.

"Oh no, Mama, I would never do anything like that, but I do have eyes. The man is pretty, and he is so kind. I know that I just met her, but I'm so happy for my big sissy. She seems to have gotten one of the good ones. Maybe the last one left," Symphony chuckled.

"I'm going to tell you like I told her. Never go looking for a man. As a woman, that is not your job. He is to find you and don't be fooled by the games that these niggas play. Your sister has them all figured out though. She's the MVP when it comes to running games on them. That child had all her bills on somebody else's auto pay." I laughed. "She was something serious before Onyx came along and sat her ass down."

"Don't tell me that, Mama. Ooooh, I can't wait to go to Atlanta. I know that I am going to have such a good time." Symphony exclaimed.

"Symphony, shut your little ass up. Don't think that you are about to go to Atlanta and run wild. These days, your ass will end up like Ebony on *The Player's Club* or with a man that plays for both teams. Atlanta is wild." We both cackled. "Come on. Let's go back in here and check on your daddy."

"Mama, doggone, he asleep. You go back in there and I'm going to head back to this office and put some work in."

"I'll call you later, Mama."

"OK, baby," I said as I got up and sauntered back to Sterling's room.

Symphony was correct. Sterling was sound asleep. Climbing into the recliner, I decided to get some rest as well. Shortly after I dosed off, I faintly heard Sterling calling Indigo's name. Not being able to make out what he was saying, I perked up and tried to listen. I knew for a fact that I heard Indigo's name. Sterling started to whimper in his sleep, so I walked over to touch and tried to soothe him.

Finally, The Truth

STERLING

Even in my sleep he wouldn't let me rest. Being in that accident and wrestling with death must have opened me up to some shit that I had no idea existed. I refused to go through the rest of my days with a dead nigga hollering at me. I've got to tell her. Struggling to open my eyes, I blurted out, "Jordan, I killed Indigo!!!!"

"I killed him. That was the only way. I knew that he wouldn't let you or I be, so I got rid of him." I confessed.

"Sterling, what the fuck are you talking about? Indigo ran off with Imani. They walked out the door at the same time. I saw it with my own eyes."

"You saw them walk out the door together but that was it, Jordan. What you didn't see was me coming from the side of the house and grabbing him. Nor did you see Solo grabbing Imani."

"Wait, the Solo that Indigo knocked out that night at the house?" Jordan confirmed.

"Yes, that Solo, Jordan. The same Solo that got his arm broke after calling you a bitch," I affirmed.

"After you told me that you were pregnant, I went to the Saxton Projects and paid Imani a visit. I offered to pay her for her help. She was with it because she was really feeling that nigga. She would have done anything to be in your shoes. She agreed and it only took a thousand dollars for her to come to your house and accuse him of being with her. In her eyes, it was a win win, she would get the man and the money. It was a hoodrat's dream come true."

"I paid Solo five thousand to come with me and help me handle business. I paid a few jits that I knew to grab their cars and take them to the chop shop. I knew that the second that Imani knocked on your door that you would lose your shit and put him out. Jordan, you did exactly what I needed you to do so that I could do what needed to be done. I killed Indigo and Solo killed Imani." I admitted and waited for Jordan to interrupt me. She didn't. She stood there stunned. Too stunned to speak so I continued.

"We took them to the woods, tied them up, wrapped them both in plastic, and shot them. If it makes it any better, there wasn't any torture involved. It was a clean hit.

After we shot them, I murked Solo. He had to go because I couldn't trust that he wouldn't run his mouth, so I offed his ass, too."

"After the deeds were done, I rushed them across town to my uncle's funeral home. I paid him ten grand to have all three cremated. My other uncle, who is now the chaplain of this hospital, was the co-owner of the funeral home. He came while we were wrapping everything up. He didn't know exactly what I'd done, but he knew it was some foul shit. Because of that, he doesn't fuck with me anymore."

"That's the real reason why it seemed like they disappeared into thin air. It's because they did, and I made sure that there was no evidence. I burned it all and threw the gun in the river. Everything went just the way that it was supposed to. Before you say anything, baby, I did this for us. I'm sorry for lying to you all of these years. I just didn't know any other way that we could be together. In my mind, I did what I had to do and back in those days, doing what I had to do was just normal."

"Say something, Jordan....Please!!!" I begged.

Jordan sat back on the bed and grabbed my hand. Leaning over me slightly, she stared into my eyes. "Sterling, I don't know what I'm supposed to say."

"Tell me what you are feeling. Are you sad, hurt, or angry? Are you upset at me? I need to know, baby."

"No."

"No. Did you say no, Jordan?"

"Yes, I said no. No, I'm not mad, upset, or any of that. I don't feel shit. If anyone were to hear this, they would probably think that I was the coldest bitch on earth but I'm glad he's gone. It didn't matter to me whether he ran off with somebody else or he ran off a cliff. I didn't give a fuck then and I don't give a fuck now. The only problem that I have with any of this is the fact that you didn't tell me earlier."

Surprised at what she's saying, I squeezed Jordan's hand and cried like a newborn. I'd been holding on to that secret for over twenty years. I'd never told anyone. In fact, I'd never muttered a single word about what I'd done again. Not even to myself. The release was more emotional that I'd expected.

"Baby, I thought that you would think that I was some kind of fucking monster. That's why I never told you. I didn't want you to look at me like you looked at him. I never wanted to do anything but love and protect you."

"I know, Sterling, I know," she said as she whispered softly in my ear.

"When you told me that Indigo put his hands on you, I couldn't take it. I wanted to fuck him up on sight. You know that I met with him that same day. I sat there in that barbershop for two hours listening to him lie to me. I listened to him tell me that he didn't know where he went

wrong in his marriage. He said that he couldn't understand why you were cold shouldering him. Then had the
nerve to say that he didn't do nothing wrong."

"Shidd, Jordan. Anybody who spent more than ten
minutes with him would have known that was a lie. We all
knew that he was fucking over you. If I could have taken
him out that day, I would have but I had to play it cool and
come up with a plan. That was not the time to make rash
decisions."

"I get that, Sterling, but I still feel like you could have
told me something. Shit, you could have said that the
Juarez brothers caught up with him and that would have
sufficed."

"Jordan, I'm sorry. Most of all, I didn't want you
carrying the burden of knowing what I'd done to Taji's
father. I loved her like she was mine and that was the only
thing that hurt me about all of this. Me being the reason
that she no longer had a father. That's why I got so pissed
when you sent her away while you were pregnant. I
wanted to be that for her. I mean, hell, that's the least that
I could do."

"Don't sweat that, baby, she had my father. He was a
great positive role model for her. He gave her all the love
and care that she could have ever needed."

"I know that your father was a great man, Baby Love,

but I wanted so long for us to be a family. A *real* family. You, me, and the girls."

My head began to swoon. "Whew, I'm getting dizzy, Jordan. I don't know if it was the medicine they had me on or what, but I need to tell you this and I don't want you to think that I am crazy."

"Boy, stop. Like I said, you can tell me anything."

"Before I came to, Indigo was talking to me. I was able to hear his voice loud and clear. I even saw him standing behind you a little while ago. He kept telling me that I needed to tell you, and he was right. I did."

"Sterling, one of the side effects of coming off the medicines is hallucinations. I'm surprised you didn't see more than Indigo. Whether it was real or it wasn't, I'm glad you told me and baby, it changes nothing. There is nothing that you could say to make me stop loving you. You know we are in this for life and your secret is safe with me. This will never leave this room."

"That is music to my ears. I just knew that you were going to get up and haul ass out of this room and leave me here looking like a crash dummy." Jordan cackled.

"I would never leave you. The way that my life got better the minute that you came in it, boy, please. I'm not going anywhere, and you aren't either. Especially now," she joked.

"Now that you are awake, and since you are in the

confessing mood, tell me about this Moné Marie chick." Jordan said as she cut her eyes at me.

I closed my eyes.

"Sterling, please don't make me kick you off in your ass. I hate to hurt a hurt man," she said as she removed her hand from mine.

"When you first moved to Atlanta, I had to stay at work late to work on a couple of new accounts. Moné Marie offered to help, and I really needed the manpower, well woman power, so I let her stay."

"Is this going where I think it's going, Sterling, because if so———."

"Wait, Jordan. Let me finish. I did not have sex with her. But she did give me head for like a minute before I made her stop. The guilt was too much for me and I didn't want to do anything to jeopardize losing you. It never happened again and since then, I put her on the second floor where I don't have to see her. It's been handled and I'm serious." I reassured.

"You are telling me that a bitch was in the process of giving you head and you stopped her? Is that what you are saying to me, Sterling?"

"Yes, Jordan. That's what I'm telling you and if I could put my right hand on a bible, I would. It went no further."

"Well hell, Baby, I've got to commend you. That's some strong ass will power and discipline that you've got because if a nigga was ever licking this monkey, he ain't stopping until his chin is dripping and it was ate off the bone."

"Jordan?!?!" I cackled and coughed. "Owwww, ouch. That shit hurt."

"I'm sorry for making you laugh but I'm just telling you the truth, baby. You know I love a good licking, don't you?" Jordan teased.

"Yes, I do but on the real. I'm sorry about that, too, but nothing like that has ever happen nor will ever happen again."

"Shiddd, I know it won't. I'm not worried about that. We are twenty-five plus years in together. Ain't nothing splitting us up. So what, you got your dick a lil wet. I can handle that but not too much though. Don't be like Indigo. I would hate to have to get my other side nigga to off you." She was smirking as she grabbed my hand and raised it to her mouth.

"See, Jordan. That's why I don't tell you shit because you are always playing."

Winking her eye at me, she stated, "Who said I was playing?"

THE END

Epilogue

JORDAN

I t'd been 2 years since Sterling's accident and while his recovery wasn't easy, he made it through. He now walked with a cane and was very self-conscious because of it, but I did my best to reassure him that he was still the sexiest muthafucka to ever walk this earth. Sterling started attending physical therapy the second that he was cleared to do so. Day in and day out, he worked tirelessly to get better, and he did. I refused to leave my husband's side while he recovered, so I moved back to Roseville permanently. I moved into the home that Sterling had purchased for us and rented out the house that Indigo and I shared. I send Taji the income from that home every month. Taji had been paying for my bills for years, thinking that I was broke. But I never touched a dime of that money. Every penny went to an account and once everything was out in the open, I sent her that back, too.

Me and Sterling were finally able to take the trip of our dreams. We booked a two weeks' vacation to Bora Bora and relaxed the entire time we were there. We ate, smoked, prayed, and I gently made love to my man while suspended over the ocean. We fell in love with each other over and over again. Things could not be better between the two of us. We've always had an exceptional love and appreciation for each other, but the accident made us even closer. We were practically joined at the hip.

The accounting firm was still running smoothly and thriving. Symphony did an amazing job running the company while her father was incapacitated. She ran a tight ship just like him and managed to bring on more accounts. In the process of her running the ship, she lost a crew member. Ms. Moné Marie resigned and signed with an accounting firm across town. Nobody gave a damn. I sure didn't and neither did Symphony. Once Sterling was well enough to return to work, Symphony decided to take up her sister's offer and visited her for two weeks. She loved it so much that she decided to move to Atlanta and finish her degree there. The townhouse that Taji purchased for me was now being occupied by Symphony. She loved the quick pace of the city, and the Atlanta nightlife was everything. She settled right in and without around, she was able to live her life on her terms. Much like her big sister once did.

Symphony had a thing for the bad boys and no longer had to hide it. Taji taught her to tread lightly and to be careful with who she dealt with. Taji and Symphony were like one in the same. Their bond was growing stronger than ever and in Symphony's eyes, Taji could do no wrong. Taji finally had someone that she didn't play about. She realized that her baby sister was a smaller version of her younger self and was doing her best to show her the ropes.

Once Symphony saw the way that her sister lived, she wanted the same for herself. I had lit a fire in her by letting it slip that Taji knew how to run game on these niggas and it was now her goal to learn everything that Taji could teach her. Taji was in the process of showing Symphony how to never end up broke and to pay these niggas dust. I knew that the minute they got together that they would be with the shits but what could I possibly do about it? They were both grown so I gave Symphony the advice that any mother would. "Be careful and watch your back."

Taji looked out for her and had introduced Symphony to a few of her favorite people. Things between the two were going well until Onyx figured out what was going on. He scolded Taji because he didn't think that it was a good idea to teach her little sister how to seduce men and get over on them. He warned her that it just wasn't smart in this day and age. Taji did what she did best. Ignored him. Because of her sister, Symphony was dating a star player for the Atlanta Falcons and was turning him out. In Taji's mind, it was a job well done.

Sterling still had nightmares about Indigo from time to time but nothing that he couldn't handle. He still stood on what he did and if he had to do it over again, he would. Nothing was going to stop him from being with the love of his life and raising his own child. What he revealed to me that day in the hospital was never brought up again. I didn't mutter another word about Indigo and that was all the proof that Sterling needed to know that he'd done the right thing. He understood that I had no heaven or hell to put him in but if things had gone bad, I could have put him away for life. Instead, I loved the idea that he protected our family the way that he did and loved him for it just that much more. Indigo was right about one thing. He was that nigga. Just not the right nigga for me.

About the Author

L. L. Momon is an emerging author of black romance, romantic suspense novels and whatever else her mind can conceive. Her imagination is boundless. Her goal is to write the kind of stories that transcends. She wants you to turn the television off and put your phone on DND. Grab your favorite blanket, a snack and tune out the world, even if it's just for a moment. Born and raised in the historical Tuskegee, Alabama, her mother can be credited for her love of romance novels. Learning to read at just four years old, she would often sneak and read books from her mother's Harlequin novel collection. While certainly not appropriate for a child, it kept her attention and was solely responsible for her love of reading. She is the author of Whittling Wood Part 1 and 2 and a Savage and His Wicked Ways. There are several other projects in the works.